RED HOT REVIEWS

"Guaranteed to hold your attention from beginning to end."
—Isaac Anderson
The New York Times

"Sometimes amusing, sometimes gruesome, and always charged with excitement."
—Elizabeth Bullock
Book Week

"Bang up thriller and excellent character study."
Saturday Review of Literature

Novels by **MARGARET MILLAR**
available in Crime Classics® editions

MARGARET MILLAR

FIRE WILL FREEZE

INTERNATIONAL POLYGONICS, LTD.
NEW YORK CITY

FIRE WILL FREEZE

Copyright ©1944 by Margaret Millar.
Copyright renewed 1971 by The Margaret Millar Survivor's
Trust u/a 4/12/82.
Reprinted with the author's permission.
Cover: Copyright ©1987 by International Polygonics, Ltd.

Library of Congress Card Catalog No. 87-80302
ISBN 0-930330-59-5

Printed and manufactured in the United States of America
by Guinn Printing.
First IPL printing April 1987.
10 9 8 7 6 5 4 3 2 1

Chapter 1

MISS ISOBEL SETON SETTLED HER CHIN INTO THE collar of her sable coat and, as was her custom in moments of stress, mentally composed an abusive letter. Her lips moved gently as she groped for a good strong beginning.

"Messrs. Abercrombie & Fitch, Sirs:
I have been mercilessly swindled by your allegedly reputable firm. Last week I purchased a pair of skis at your store for the sum of seventy-five dollars. I intimated to the man in charge that I had never been on skis before. He assured me that it was all a matter of keeping your knees bent. If this man is an example of your staff, well, all I can say is I'd like to bend his knees for him . . ."

"Too personal," Miss Seton murmured critically into her collar. "I shall have to be more curt."

"Sirs:
I am returning to you, via dog-sled, a pair of skis for which I foolishly paid you seventy-five dollars on January the fourteenth. I feel your staff should have more responsibility to the general public than to sell skis to anyone simply for the asking. I do not mind being mercilessly swindled, having lived in New York for ten years, but I object strongly to lack of civic responsibility.

"Because one of your irresponsible clerks did not prevent me from buying a pair of skis, I am sitting here in what these damned Canadians call a Sno-bus, which means a bus that meets a Sno-train and conveys one to a Sno-lodge. I am marooned in the wilds of Quebec in a raging Sno-storm. My nose is red. I am thirty-five, which is not an age for adjustments. I am hungry. The

7

bus driver has pimples at the back of his neck. The windows are frozen and I am cooped up with several other unfortunates, none of whom had even the foresight to bring along stimulants . . ."

"Oh, dear," Miss Seton muttered. "I *will* get personal."

In the seat behind, the honeymoon couple resumed the argument they had begun in the station at Montreal. The woman's voice was loud and tearful.

"A honeymoon on skis! Why not a motorcycle? Or a submarine?"

"Now, angel," the man said. "Now, Maudie."

"Angel be damned," Maudie said.

"Now . . ."

"You be damned too."

Miss Seton, in the act of some wholesale damnation herself, felt a twinge of sympathy. She moved her ear a fraction of an inch closer to the top of the seat.

"This is the worst honeymoon I ever had, Herbert," Maudie said. "Just look at the class of people I've got to associate with. Just look around, Herbert."

Miss Seton shrank into her sables while Herbert presumably looked around.

"Outdoor types," Maudie continued. "I bet they can hardly wait for their vitamins."

"Vitamins," Herbert said cautiously, "are all right."

"The Riviera with Tom, Bermuda with poor Jack, and a *snow bus* with you, Herbert. Well, I won't say any more. It speaks for itself."

Under pretext of moving into a more comfortable position, Miss Seton maneuvered her head until her eyes were on a level with the top of the seat.

Herbert was studiously pretending to be admiring the scenery though the windows were completely opaque. Even in anguish his face bore the stamp of good nature. It was fat and pink and scrubbed-looking and seemed uncertain whether to cry or laugh. He wore a corduroy visored ski-cap which covered his head and ears.

"I'll bet he's as bald as an egg," Miss Seton thought, and turned her attention to Maudie.

Maudie was sniffling into a damp half-frozen handkerchief. Miss Seton had a glimpse of a tiny tear-drenched face, large mournful blue eyes and wisps of pale gold hair straggling from beneath a white fur parka. Apparently at some time in the past Maudie had not been averse to a ski honeymoon for she had gone to some trouble to trick herself out as elegantly as possible. Her ski-suit was pale blue suede sprouting white fur.

Deeply ashamed of her sable coat and Sally Victor hat Miss Seton smiled apologetically at Herbert and ducked her head. Above the howling of the wind she heard Herbert's voice saying hopefully:

"See, Maudie? I bet she's not full of vitamins."

"She's full of prunes," Maudie said distinctly.

Miss Seton was moved by this injustice. "I haven't eaten a prune since I left boarding school fifteen years ago," she murmured. "Fifteen years. Oh, dear."

She was so dispirited by this thought that she changed position again, this time moving well forward in her seat. It was much more difficult to catch anything the couple in front of her said. When they talked at all it was in whispers. Usually it was the man who talked and the girl did not look at him but sat fumbling with her purse or pushing her hands in and out of the pockets of her jacket.

Her nervous movements did not fit in with the calm, poised expression on her face or the easy way she wore her well-used ski-suit. She had pushed her hood back on her head and the bright red cloth made her hair seem blue-black and her skin too dead white.

"I wonder why she's so pale," Miss Seton thought, and moved her head again to look up at the rack where the girl's skis were placed. The skis, like the ski-suit, were well-used, and had once been, Miss Seton decided, expensive. On the rack beside the skis lay the girl's bag, and that too seemed out of place. It was very new and very cheap.

Her name was Paula, Miss Seton knew. The man said the name often, as if the name itself fascinated him, quite apart from the fact that it belonged to the girl. Even though he spoke in whispers he sounded angry.

". . . regret it, Paula."

The girl shrugged and said nothing. Miss Seton hurriedly twitched the veil away from her ears and bent forward a little more. But the wind had risen again and was rattling the window panes. By the time it had abated the man was talking about christianias and stem turns. His voice was louder now and he turned his head around and gave Miss Seton a long cold stare. Miss Seton blushed and bent over to examine an imaginary run in her stocking.

"What a savage-looking creature," she said to herself. "Probably suckled by werewolves."

She studied his profile with renewed interest. It was a rugged profile topped by a thatch of red hair clipped very short. The only non-rugged thing about the young man was his eyelashes, which were long and curly, and of which, Miss Seton judged from the furious way he blinked them, he was very much ashamed.

Miss Seton withdrew into her collar and wrote him a letter.

> "Dear Werewolf:
> I haven't eaten a prune since I left boarding school fifteen years ago. This may seem irrelevant, but I wanted to give you some idea of my state of mind. I have just been looking at your eyelashes and find them entrancing. Are you married, by the way? I'm not so bad. I have brown hair and brown eyes. I'm thirty-five and I have a modest income. . . ."

"No, I mustn't propose," Miss Seton murmured dreamily. The werewolf was far too young anyway and probably on the verge of marrying or the verge of divorcing Paula. Nothing else could account for the intensity of his gaze, Miss Seton decided, unless he was a communist! Or perhaps he merely belonged to the intense type of youth, as opposed to the bored-since-birth variety like the girl across the aisle.

This other girl's luggage was conspicuously new, conspicuously expensive and conspicuously labeled, "Miss Joyce Hunter, Westmount, Quebec." Like the tearful Maudie and the poised Paula, Joyce Hunter was dressed for skiing. She wore a suit of white Grenfell cloth and from the edge of her parka grew three black shiny curls as bored and perfect as Joyce herself.

Joyce's perfection was merely visual, however. As far as Miss Seton knew, the girl could not talk. Throughout the trip she had sat in perfect silence, yawning delicately now and then, running her eyes over the other occupants of the bus without the faintest flicker of interest. Witnessing such deadly boredom made Miss Seton sleepy and she closed her eyes only to open them again quickly when Joyce uttered her first words of the day.

"Damn and blast, Poppa," she said. "I broke a fingernail."

So the man with her *was* her father, Miss Seton thought, pleased with herself. She had had nothing more to go on than the fact that Mr. Hunter looked paternal. He had white hair and he wore a harassed and worried expression, as if he was anxious to be friendly with his daughter and didn't know how to begin. Miss Seton was glad to note that his skis were as bright and unused as her own and that he too wore civilian clothes and didn't look any too happy at finding himself on a Sno-bus.

"In fact," Miss Seton said softly, "none of us looks very happy. I thought skiers were a jovial lot, always singing and thumping each other on the back."

Perhaps the thumping would come later after they'd all had a couple of christianias, but the chances didn't look bright. Suppose Herbert thumped the werewolf, it seemed probable that the werewolf would in turn thump Herbert right into heaven. And suppose she herself thumped Joyce . . .

She peered past the perfect Hunter profile and met Mr. Hunter's eyes. He seemed to be aware, with the intuition of parents, that Miss Seton was having unflattering ideas about his daughter. He frowned slightly and turned his head away.

"Joyce," he said.

Joyce blinked long black eyelashes to indicate that she recognized her name.

"Joyce, are you quite comfortable? Not too cold?"

Joyce blinked again to indicate that she was or she wasn't, who cared. Miss Seton smiled slightly and maliciously at Mr. Hunter and closed her eyes. She wrote a brief, forceful note:

"Dear Mr. Hunter:
You lack firmness and oomph. If you feel incapable of working up these qualities I shall be glad to assist. Is your wife living, by the way? I have brown hair, brown eyes and a modest income . . ."

"There I go again," Miss Seton said critically. "Thirty-five *is* a dangerous age."

In the seat behind, Maudie blew her nose and started again from the beginning.

"I know you're forty-three, Herbert. I know you're twenty pounds overweight and you've always wanted to ski and if you don't learn now you never will. I know all that. But what I say is, so what?"

"But you said you wanted to come, Maudie," Herbert said. "You said you'd never been in Quebec."

"So what?" There was a grim satisfaction in Maudie's voice as if she had found exactly the right phrase and intended to go on using it. "So what, Herbert?"

"You said it would be kind of cosy, Maudie, just the two of us in front of an open fire."

"Produce the open fire, Herbert," Maudie said ominously.

"It will come."

"We are already hours late."

"One hour," Herbert said faintly.

"Hours."

"One hour."

"I'm on your side, Herbert," Miss Seton murmured. "One hour."

"Hours!" Maudie yelled. "You can't call me a liar and get away with it!"

"Oh yes he can," Miss Seton whispered into her collar.

Even Joyce Hunter was roused to interest. She moved her head languidly, passed her eyes over Maudie and Herbert and Miss Seton, and turned away.

"Poppa. Cigarette."

Mr. Hunter leaped to obey. He fumbled in the pockets of his tweed topcoat and brought out a cigarette case and a lighter.

"No," Joyce said.

Maudie's influence was making itself felt. "No *what?*" Mr. Hunter cried irritably.

"Poppa!"

"Sorry, dear."

"Don't like that kind."

"Sorry. They're all I've got."

Joyce sighed and resumed her contemplation of nothing. Mr. Hunter attempted to melt some of the ice from the window with his bare hand. Miss Seton saw the huge ruby on his third finger and thought, "With my modest income too . . . ."

She went to sleep with her head resting against the rattling window and a cold wind blowing down her neck.

From his seat behind the Hunters' Mr. Anthony Goodwin watched Miss Seton's head sink lower and lower and gradually relax on her breast. Mr. Goodwin was filled with the profound bitterness found only in an insomniac contemplating a sleeping fellow human.

Mr. Goodwin's mind seethed with chaotic monosyllables. "God. Sleep. Death. Rest. Hell."

Nor was Mr. Goodwin's body any better adapted to snobusses than his mind. There was no adequate space for his long and intense limbs. "Cribbed, cabined, confined," Mr. Goodwin mumbled. "Cramped. Creased. Cold. Crushed. Crapulent." When he stretched his legs he hit his ankle sharply against the stone-cold heater attached to the seat ahead. When he leaned back to rest his head it forced his hat down over his forehead. Finally he removed the hat, jerked his legs under him, closed his eyes, and tried to imitate Miss Seton. But while Miss Seton's body followed the joltings of the bus like that of an experienced horsewoman, Mr. Goodwin teetered back and forth clinging desperately to the arm of the seat and to something else, something as soft and malleable as a woman's hand.

"Well, dearie," said the owner of the hand, "if you want to wrestle, you wrestle. It's all right with me."

Mr. Goodwin flung the hand away, he rolled his head back and grimaced at the ceiling of the bus. Then he waved his long arms wildly in apology.

"Well, say, you needn't throw a fit. My name's Morning, Miss Gracie Morning. What's yours?"

Mr. Goodwin had been on the defensive against Miss Morning ever since she entered the bus. She had stood in the doorway, smiling impartially and cheerfully at all the occupants. Then, impelled by the fate which had dogged Mr. Goodwin's footsteps for years, Miss Morning had singled him out, clambered past his legs and sat down beside him with a box of chocolates, a copy of *Secrets* and a strong urge to talk. So far Mr. Goodwin had avoided giving her an opening by shutting his eyes and mumbling to himself.

"If the woman has any sense," Mr. Goodwin muttered, "she will know I am *thinking* and do not care to be disturbed."

"I didn't get the name," Miss Morning said pleasantly.

"Goodwin."

"English, are you?"

"Yes."

"Fancy that! Refugee?"

Miss Morning peered around Mr. Goodwin's elbow. Mr. Goodwin had a glimpse of vividly bronze hair and blue eyes, and a whiff of some primitive scent.

"No," he said.

"Going to ski?"

"Yes."

"What do you do for a living?"

"I . . ." Mr. Goodwin groaned and slapped his forehead smartly. To Mr. Goodwin's friends this would have indicated that he was having an idea and couldn't be bothered. Miss Morning simply thought he was a little crazy.

"Well look, Goodwin," she said kindly, "if you don't want to tell me you don't have to. Though as far as that goes I'm no squawker. I wouldn't tell a soul. Why, I got friends in some of the damnedest rackets you ever heard of. I know a guy back in Toronto, that's my home town, who eats beer bottles for ten bucks apiece. No kidding." Miss Morning patted her red curls and smoothed the bright blue feathers on her hat. "I bet I look a fright."

"You look anything but a fright," Mr. Goodwin said stoically.

"In my profession we got to look our best," Miss Morning confided. "The men expect it."

Mr. Goodwin's mouth moved horribly.

"Now don't you go getting ideas," Miss Morning said with a broad smile. "You men are all alike, even the nice young ones like you. I can read you like a book. Mind if I call you Goodie?"

"I mind intensely," Mr. Goodwin replied, but his voice was lost in the howling of the wind.

"I dance."

"Ah?"

"Sure. I've got a little number called Knit to Fit. I come out wearing a bathing suit, see, and I bounce around a little and then the suit gets caught on something, maybe a gentleman's watch fob, and it unravels, only not all of it. Pretty good, eh?"

"Marvelous," Mr. Goodwin bleated.

"But maybe you'll see me. I might get a chance to do it at the lodge. You going to be there long?"

"No. Oh, no."

"Too bad. I'm *crazy* about fair men. Say, your teeth are chattering. Are you cold?"

"Yes."

"That's one advantage of my profession," Miss Morning said cheerfuly. "You get toughened up. I never mind the cold any more. Boy, it sure was hard at first with nothing but a G-string between me and ammonia."

Mr. Goodwin folded his arms over his chest and repeated this sentence bleakly to himself. It conveyed nothing to him.

In the seat ahead Joyce Hunter burst, incongruously, into giggles.

"Poppa."

"Yes?" Mr. Hunter's voice was cold.

"I bet you can hardly wait."

"I beg your pardon?"

"You'll be *bristling* with watch fobs, Poppa!"

"Joyce!"

"What's a G-string?"

Mr. Hunter cleared his throat. "It is, I believe, some— some sort of apparatus used to camouflage the female form. I don't wish to discuss it."

A hand tapped his shoulder and he turned his head irritably and found himself staring into Miss Morning's eyes.

"I say," Miss Morning said. "You got the time? My watch stopped."

Mr. Hunter blushed painfully and reached for his watch. "Exactly four-thirty-six."

Joyce giggled again.

"Thanks." Miss Morning returned to her pursuit of Mr. Goodwin. "Nice old guy, isn't he? I'm *crazy* about older men, especially if they got white hair. I don't know, it sort of gets me. I wonder who the dead-panned dame is."

"His daughter. She calls him Poppa."

Miss Morning chuckled. "That doesn't mean a thing, Goodie. If all the guys I've called Poppa were laid end to end . . ."

Mr. Goodwin struck his forehead again and said, "Spare me. Spare me the apodosis."

"What's that?"

"Spare me the end of that sentence. I don't think I could bear to hear the results of having all the men you've called Poppa laid end to end."

"Say, you *are* a funny guy." Miss Morning's voice was anxious. "What's your racket?"

"I write," Mr. Goodwin said belligerently. "I write *poetry*. I am a *poet*."

"Well, you needn't get tough about it. I didn't say anything about poets. As a matter of fact, I'm crazy about poets." Miss Morning retired rather huffily to her second layer of chocolates.

Joyce Hunter whispered, "I say, Poppa."

"Yes?"

"Did you hear that? He's Goodwin, the poet, Anthony Goodwin."

"Is he? I never read poetry."

"Well, naturally not. Neither do I. But he's supposed to be terribly debauched. Lies around in a drunken stupor. I read it in *Time*."

"I don't think," Mr. Hunter said dryly, "that he can debauch Miss Morning."

"Well, there's me. I think he's rather cute. Too bad he's traveling with his mother."

"His mother?" Mr. Hunter said in surprise.

"The fat lady in the back seat."

Mr. Hunter turned his head, and there, sure enough, was a fat lady occupying the whole of the left back seat. She wore an immense raccoon coat and it was impossible to tell how much of the lady was coat and how much sheer lady. At any rate the seat was full. The lady was gently snoring.

"I can't understand you, Joyce," Mr. Hunter said crossly. "One minute you're in a coma and the next minute you're ferreting out other people's private lives."

"Well, that's just my way," Joyce said modestly. She turned her head and looked again at the fat lady in the raccoon coat. She added thoughtfully, "Of course she may *not* be his mother at all. She may just look old enough to be his mother because he's debauched her so thoroughly."

"Oh, Lord," Mr. Hunter said with a sigh.

"Well, you just wait and see!"

Silence descended upon the Hunters and Joyce relapsed into her coma.

In the back seat the raccoon coat began to twitch and the gentle snoring ceased and Mrs. Evaline Vista returned to consciousness, pleasantly unaware that her morals had been slandered.

She yawned loudly, and stretched, and thought what an excellent idea it was to sleep away the trip and what an excellent idea the trip itself was. It would do Anthony, and Anthony's poetry, a world of good. Anthony had had too much pampering; he needed to face the world and battle the elements. He needed, in one word, Mrs. Vista's favorite word, *virility*.

"Ah, virility," Mrs. Vista whispered, rather sadly, for she had suffered from it, in her day. Mr. Cecil Vista had had far too much of it. His last trip to Brighton with his secretary had cost him ten thousand pounds a year alimony. It was only fitting that Mrs. Vista should use the ten thousand pounds to inject into the arts some of Cecil's own quality.

She studied the back of Anthony's head fondly. What a good thing it was that innocent unworldly geniuses had a Mrs. Vista.

She said, "Anthony!"

Mr. Goodwin turned sharply. "Ah, Evaline. So you're awake."

"Where's your hat, Anthony?"

"On my lap."

"You'll catch pneumonia. Put it on instantly."

By way of answer Mr. Goodwin jammed the hat savagely down over his ears. It was a green felt Tyrolean hat with an orange feather growing from the band. Mr. Goodwin looked and felt extremely silly in it, but it had been a present from Mrs. Vista who had bought it in Bavaria for Cecil. Cecil had refused to wear it, so Mrs. Vista gave it to Anthony. She had, at times, an economical turn of mind.

"There," said Mrs. Vista in her comfortable bellow. "Much better. Oh, driver! Driver! Are we nearly there?"

The driver took his eyes off the road for a fraction of a second. "Few more miles to go."

He had a slight accent. A French-Canadian, Mrs. Vista decided, and was immediately impelled to heave herself out of her seat and stagger the few steps to the front of the bus. She fell into the seat opposite Paula and the red-haired young man and settled down to engage the bus driver in conversation. She had never talked to a French-Canadian and she thought it probable that French-Canadian culture could do with a jog.

"A very bumpity road," she said pleasantly. "Is there any danger, do you suppose?"

The driver did not turn around. He had pulled his hat down and his coat collar up and his voice came out, muffled: "One of my tire chains is loose."

There did seem to be a queer, clanking noise, Mrs. Vista agreed.

"I may have to adjust it," the driver said. "I thought it would hold out but it will not." He raised his voice. "Please remain in your seats, everyone. We are stopping for a minute."

The bus lurched to a stop. The driver squirmed out of his seat and wrenched the door open. A blast of fine sharp snow like tiny particles of steel was blown into the open door. It cut into Mrs. Vista's face and stung her to tears.

"Driver!" she shouted, covering her face with her hands.

From the back of the bus Maudie Thropple's sharp high voice demanded, "What's wrong? Where's he going?"

Mrs. Vista shouted, "Driver!" again, but the door had closed and the wind howled against it with impotent rage.

Miss Seton woke up and rubbed her neck. The warmth of her head had cleaned the ice from a small circle of window. She blinked gently and looked out. The snow had drifted, curved and sharp like scimitars, along the fences. She saw the driver plod past the window with his head bent against the wind.

She leaned forward and tapped the red-haired young man on the shoulder.

"What's the matter?" she asked.

The young man scowled and said, "He's just going to fix something."

"Oh." Miss Seton smiled with relief. "I'm Isobel Seton.

I suppose we're all going to the same place and might as well get acquainted."

"Chad Ross," the young man said. "And this is Paula . . ."

"Lashley," the girl said quickly. "Paula Lashley."

They both turned away. Feeling properly snubbed Miss Seton looked at Mrs. Vista.

"It's the tire chains," Mrs. Vista said loudly. "Don't get excited, anyone. He's simply gone to fix the chains."

Joyce Hunter snapped back to consciousness.

"Well, why doesn't he?"

Every eye in the bus turned simultaneously to the back window, but like the others it was frozen solid.

"He's been gone," Joyce said calmly, "exactly five minutes. I've been counting. I don't think it should take more than one minute to reach the chains, and if he's fixing them why don't we hear something?"

"Because you're talking too much," Mr. Hunter said irritably. "It's all nonsense."

Joyce smiled patiently and did not answer. The others were silent, staring at her, listening intently for any signs of the driver.

"I *hope*," Joyce said affably, after a time, "there are no wolves."

"You silly girl," Mrs. Vista said, just as affably.

Without a word Joyce went to the back window and began rubbing it with her handkerchief. She paid no attention to the man occupying the seat, though he watched her with quiet amusement.

The others had broken into excited conversation about wolves. Miss Seton stepped into the aisle and stretched her arms.

"I should be very surprised to see a wolf," she murmured. "Very surprised."

Joyce turned around. "Well, *I* shouldn't be surprised. I happen to know you're an American."

Miss Seton nodded guiltily.

"And you wouldn't know about wolves in Canada. Canada is teeming with wolves."

Miss Seton conceded the wolves but refused to lose faith in the bus-driver. "He may be having more difficulty than he . . ."

"Look out," Joyce said grimly, pointing to the small space she had cleared with her handkerchief. "Come and look out."

Miss Seton walked to the back of the bus and looked out.

The bus-driver had disappeared.

Chapter 2

"HE SEEMS," MISS SETON ANNOUNCED IN A WEAK voice, pressing her nose right up against the pane, "to be gone."

The man in the back seat removed Miss Seton's sable-covered elbow from his ribs and said dryly, "Would you mind? I'm rather ticklish."

Miss Seton looked down into a pair of amused brown eyes shaded by the brim of a gray fedora. Against the gray of his hat and overcoat, the man's skin was deeply tanned and leathery. His mouth was twisted in a rather cynical half-smile.

"My name's Charles Crawford," he said. "Remember me as Charles Crawford, a *very* ticklish man."

"The bus-driver," Miss Seton said coldly, "has disappeared."

"Well?" Mr. Crawford said. "What do you want me to do?"

"Nothing at all." Miss Seton turned away, blushing slightly. Obviously Mr. Crawford was not one of those people who are helpful in a crisis, if there was a crisis. A city slicker, she decided, who got his tan under a sun lamp and stood around making small talk.

Still, he looked competent—more competent than the other men in the bus. She glanced worriedly at the cluster of men standing in the aisle talking. Neither Mr. Hunter nor Mr. Herbert Thropple would be capable of taking charge in an emergency. They were both good substantial citizens, but they couldn't even manage their respective women. Mr. Goodwin was probably, if the magazine was correct, drunk, or if not drunk, crazy. As for the red-haired Chad Ross, he looked as though he was impatiently waiting for the rest of the bus to be devoured by wolves.

Miss Gracie Morning's voice rose above the babble:

"Give the fellow time. Maybe he's taking a walk or something."

"Taking a walk?" Maudie said shrilly. "In this blizzard?"

"Well, you never can tell," said Miss Morning, who had

met many strange people in her short life and had learned not to be surprised.

"This is so stupid!" Joyce cried with a withering glance around the group. "Here we are in a serious situation and all we do is talk! The driver has gone. Why should he disappear in a raging blizzard with no place to disappear to? What is there to talk about? We'll have to follow him, *now*, before the snow fills in his tracks."

None of the others had thought of this possibility. A pregnant silence descended, broken finally by Miss Seton.

She said in a quiet voice, "If we wait much longer we won't have any choice. The driver must have gone some place. If we follow him now, we'll be able to reach the same place. If we wait we'll have to stay here in the bus all night."

"Why?" Charles Crawford demanded lazily from the back seat.

"Talk, talk, talk," Joyce said scathingly. "He's been gone fifteen minutes now."

"Perhaps Mr. Crawford has a suggestion," Miss Seton said.

"Well," Mr. Crawford said, "I *have* driven busses."

Mrs. Vista beamed in the direction of Mr. Crawford. "Splendid! I knew everything would come right in the end. 'There is a tide in the affairs of men . . .' "

"Evaline," Mr. Goodwin said sadly, "it is bourgeois to quote Shakespeare."

"You can?" Miss Seton said sharply to Mr. Crawford. "You think you can drive it?"

"Of course," said Mr. Crawford.

"Hadn't you better hurry then? The snow may be drifting over the road."

Mr. Crawford rose from his seat. The others fell back to let him pass. He seated himself behind the wheel and reached for the ignition.

"And what," Joyce inquired with gentle irony, "if the driver comes back and finds us gone? He may freeze to death. I think we're making a terrible mistake and I'll bet two to one that Mr. Crawford couldn't drive a *camel*."

"True," said Mr. Crawford. The engine began to roar and Mrs. Vista began to roar too, encouraging it.

The others sat on the edge of their seats waiting for the lurch forward. The lurch came, and another, and another, and the bus was a few yards closer to the Chateau Neige. The engine raced and sputtered into silence.

Mr. Crawford removed his hat and Miss Seton could see that he was sweating and his hands were clenched tightly on the steering wheel, almost desperately.

Queer, Miss Seton thought. In an interval between lurches she moved up the aisle and took the front seat beside Mrs. Vista. Though the bus was extremely cold she saw that Mr. Crawford had unbuttoned his overcoat. *Lurch.* Mr. Crawford's overcoat pocket swung and struck the back of his seat. There was a clang of metal, barely noticeable over the roar of the engine.

He has a gun, Miss Seton thought, and the whole scene became suddenly unreal—the blizzard, the missing driver, Mr. Crawford bent over the wheel with his breath coming out of his mouth like puffs of smoke, the gun in his pocket . . .

Lurch. The engine died again and Mr. Crawford's mouth moved in silent cursing.

"I think that settles it." Joyce's voice rang out clearly through the bus.

"Shut up!" Mr. Crawford said savagely. He tried the engine again but it was dead for good this time. He put his head down on his arm for a second and Miss Seton saw that his face was the color of putty and the sweat stood out on his forehead like little drops of oil.

No one spoke while he silently put on his hat and re-buttoned his overcoat and got out from behind the wheel.

He said at last in a soft voice, "The little lady wins."

There was another silence. Then Joyce said crisply, "We'd better get started. We'll have to leave all the luggage behind."

Maudie began to weep. "I can't! Oh, I can't! We may freeze . . ."

"Hush, angel," Herbert said masterfully. "Give me your hand."

"Let go of me!"

"Do you want to stay here and die?"

"Yes!" Maudie shrieked.

"Well, all right," Herbert said, and strode into the aisle and up to the door.

"Coming, Goodwin?" said Mr. Hunter.

Mr. Goodwin leaped up, struck his head sharply against the baggage rack and joined Herbert at the door.

"Come, Evaline," he said to Mrs. Vista.

Mrs. Vista stared at him, annoyed. "Anthony, you don't mean to say you're going out into that storm with your weak chest? You must be crazy!"

Mr. Goodwin was always flattered by any aspersions cast on his sanity. He said almost gently, "Genius is to madness near allied. Come."

The door swung open and the wind trumpeted in. Herbert

stepped out and sank in snow up to his knees. He cupped his mouth with his hand and yelled, "Hurry up! The tracks are nearly gone! Make it snappy!"

Miss Morning scrambled out into the aisle and gave Maudie a good-natured push in the back. "Make it snappy, he says, dearie."

Maudie swung round and glared at her. "You take your hands off me!"

"Phooey," said Miss Morning pleasantly and followed Miss Seton and Joyce to the door.

Mr. Crawford was the last to leave. He watched the others carefully as they passed him.

There's no danger from any of them, he thought. Bad luck for me, but they're all harmless. I'll just have to be more cautious. *But what a filthy break!*

He stepped out of the door and closed it behind him. He was barely conscious of the intense cold and the blinding wind. He was accustomed to both, and his mind was working too fast to permit him to feel discomfort.

Ahead of him Miss Seton tottered through the drifts, her eyes nearly closed. The wind needled her eyelids and stung them to tears which she wiped off with her stiffening gloves. There was nothing to see and the roar of the wind was so loud there was nothing to hear. It was as if she was alone in a torture box with walls of wind, and sharp little knives of snow were being hurled from all sides.

Her face was a dull steady ache and her legs in silk stockings were numbed. When she leaned over a little she could see tracks ahead of her, and slightly to the right of these, a single set of footprints growing fainter and fainter as she moved, the footprints of the bus-driver.

"Where could he have gone?" she gasped. "And why? *"Why?"*

She stopped a moment to put her sleeve against her throbbing forehead. Her coat was thick with snow but the sleeve felt warm against her skin. I'm freezing, she thought wildly, I'm already frozen.

Then suddenly and miraculously the wind and snow vanished, as if a hole had opened in the sky and sucked them up and closed again. The silence was so sudden that she heard her own gasp of surprise and the heavy breathing of Mr. Crawford behind her. And she could see again; the bandages of snow had been lifted from her eyes, and in spite of the approaching dusk she saw everything with a new clarity and perspective—a column of strangers following some faint tracks in the snow: Mrs. Vista an enormous raccoon clinging to Mr. Goodwin's coat, Mr. Goodwin taking off his hat and carefully shaking the snow from it, Mr. Hunter wiping his frosted mustache with a handkerchief, Paula Lashley standing beside Chad Ross, still not looking at him but staring out across the snow.

Joyce Hunter was gazing around her with evident satisfaction as if she had personally ordered God to do this little favor and He had obeyed.

Miss Seton looked at her and giggled. Joyce turned in her direction and shouted, "Are you all right? You're not hysterical?" Her voice rang out sharply in the new intense silence.

In spite of her stiff cracked lips Miss Seton managed a murderous smile. "No, I'm not hysterical, Miss . . . ?"

"Hunter," Joyce said.

"Seton," Miss Seton shouted.

Paula said quietly, "I think there's a house over there."

"A house!" Maudie Thropple gave a long shuddering sigh and swooned comfortably against Herbert. "A house. We're saved."

"Saved!" Mrs. Vista echoed.

Joyce casually flicked the snow from three curls at the top of her parka and remarked that there had never been any danger anyway and it seemed silly to get all emotional because they'd seen a house. She herself, she added, had known from the first that there'd be a house.

Miss Seton looked around carefully. The house lay some five hundred yards to the east, a huge square pile of gray stone squatting on a small hill. A thin scraggly wisp of smoke issued from one chimney straight up into the sky.

It's the only place, Miss Seton thought. He must have gone there. There's nothing else.

Yet she hesitated. The footprints had disappeared now as if they had never existed. There was only a smooth unbroken field of snow in front of them, serene and inhuman. *Inhuman,* Miss Seton thought with a shiver. I can't believe a man walked there.

Chad Ross was leading the way towards the house, his long legs moving in slow rhythm through the drifts. No one was talking, they were straining towards the house because it was very cold again. For a few minutes after the wind had lifted they were warm by contrast and from excitement, but now their faces were aching. The fine laughlines around Miss Seton's eyes deepened and became static.

Awful, she thought. Why would people live here? Or did people live here? Perhaps the house was inhabited by snow creatures, white wind-bloated ghosts which skimmed the snow and left no marks.

I am hysterical, she thought, the girl was right. I'm too old to cope with ghosts. I must think of something else.

Mr. Goodwin was directly in front of her so she thought about him and wondered where he got the strange hat with the feather. She kept looking at the feather to keep from thinking about the cold and the dreary-looking house ahead of them.

There was a queer sharp noise and the feather disappeared from Mr. Goodwin's hat as precisely and quickly as if it had been shot off.

Shot off, Miss Seton repeated to herself.

She became aware that the others had stopped almost simultaneously and that Mr. Goodwin's hands were fumbling towards his head. His voice, slightly cracked and husky, came to her ears:

"Someone is shooting at me."

Mrs. Vista sat down abruptly in the snow. A second sharp crack splintered the silence.

"Down!" Charles Crawford yelled. "Keep down, everybody!"

Miss Seton's knees were fluid and she sank gratefully down. She looked around at Charles Crawford and saw that he was the only one left standing and that he seemed to be doing his best to be murdered. He had taken off his hat and was waving it violently in the air. He didn't look at all frightened or desperate as he had when he was trying to start the bus. He simply looked angry, and at the same time a little amused.

We must look like a pack of fools, Miss Seton thought. Close beside her, Miss Morning's voice whispered, "Well, I'll be damned. They must think we're somebody else."

Miss Seton raised her head a little and peered towards the house again. A light flickered for a moment in one of the windows on the second floor, and something white moved past the window. Like a ghost, Miss Seton thought, and closed her eyes very tightly and painfully.

Behind her Charles Crawford spoke again. "It's all right now, I think, but I suggest we take it slow and keep down as much as possible. Move on, up there!"

Chad Ross, still at the head of the column, turned his head and scowled, but he started walking anyway with Paula Lashley close behind him. When they were within twenty yards of the house the front door began to open slowly and cautiously and a head appeared in the crack. It stayed there, motionless, for a full minute.

Mrs. Vista put up her hand and shouted, "Ahoy! Ahoy there! We're lost!"

A sharp cackle of laughter bounced over the snow and a small squat figure came out of the door. She was dressed in black except for the white cap she wore on her head. She stood still on the snow-covered veranda, laughing.

Miss Seton shivered and turned to Charles Crawford. He had his hat back on and was watching the figure on the veranda with narrowed eyes.

"I don't like the sound of that laugh," Miss Seton whispered.

He smiled, too quickly. "Well, do I?" He raised his voice. "Move on, up there!"

It was not Chad Ross who moved first this time, it was Mrs. Vista. She plunged through the snow, wheezing and shouting, "Ahoy!" The rest followed her slowly. She waited for them at the bottom of the veranda steps and when they reached the steps they found out why.

The lady in black was not laughing, but crying. The tears were sliding down each side of her thick white nose. She did not brush them off but stood watching the people clustered at the foot of the steps, her mouth drawn back from her big white teeth, her black eyes impassive behind the tears. She had a shawl over her shoulders clutched together at the front by bony hands that were slightly dirty.

For a minute no one spoke at all except Mrs. Vista, who kept wheezing, "Ahoy!" in a faint whisper as if she were hypnotized.

Miss Seton looked at Charles Crawford, expecting him to step up and take charge as he had before. But Mr. Crawford had no intention of taking charge, apparently. He stood with his hands in his pockets, scuffing the snow with his feet.

The other men seemed equally at a loss, and Joyce Hunter had passed into another coma.

That, Miss Seton thought savagely, leaves *me*.

She shouldered her way past Mrs. Vista, looked firmly at the lady in black, and said, "Hello."

It wasn't the most brilliant beginning but it had its effect. The lady stopped crying and said, in a voice soft and husky from tears:

"You are lost?"

"No, we are not lost," Miss Seton said crisply. "We have lost our driver."

"Driver?"

"The driver of the bus we were in."

"Bus?"

"The bus that goes to the Chateau Neige," Miss Seton explained. "The driver got out and left us. He came here. We followed him."

"Here?" The lady raised one shoulder and brushed off her cheeks with her shawl. "How sad. How very *sad*."

"We . . ." Miss Seton's voice cracked and she looked angrily around at the others. "Why doesn't somebody *else* say something?"

Mr. Hunter carefully cleared his throat and said, "We are very cold. May we come inside? I'm afraid we'll freeze."

The lady in black made a clucking noise with her tongue. "It is a mild day, an extremely mild day. We have had an extremely mild winter." Her black eyes rested speculatively on them, one after another, until they came to Maudie. "That thin one there, she will freeze. There's no blood in her."

Maudie gave a little shriek and clung to Herbert. "Oh, take me away!"

"She is already freezing," the lady said, and her eyes moved on to the others. Quite suddenly she began to cry again and backed away towards the open door, moaning, "I don't want you here. Harry, you go away. I don't want you here. This is my house, my house. Go away, you thieves."

Miss Morning had had enough. She thrust her way past the others and walked aggressively up the steps of the veranda. When she spoke her voice was surprisingly gentle:

"Nobody's going to hurt you. We want to get warm. We wouldn't hurt you."

The woman backed away from her and made another swipe at her tears with her shawl.

"I haven't room," she whined. "I don't want you in my house. There are so many of us already."

Miss Seton had recovered herself. She followed Miss Morning up the steps and said briskly, "The driver is here, of course?"

"No, no, no one is here but me and my dear friends."

"Your—friends?"

"My dear friends Floraine and Etienne and Suzanne— don't you go in there!" she shouted at Miss Morning who was already inside the door. "You thief! Stealing from a poor lady. Poor Miss Rudd. Poor old lady."

She followed Miss Morning inside. Miss Seton rather hesi-
tantly went inside after her.

The hall was dim, with a high gilt ceiling. It smelled of
must and rotting woodwork and stale food. An immense
marble and brass staircase led up to the second floor, and
on the first landing of the staircase a huge yellow cat stood
waving its tail in the air.

"Hi, puss," said Miss Morning.

Miss Rudd moved close to her and touched her arm.
"My dear friend, Etienne," she said softly. "Come, Etienne.
Etienne, come here."

The cat arched his back and spat. Then, with a last wave
of his tail he stalked up the stairs.

Miss Rudd kept calling him softly, walking slowly towards the stairs.

The others were coming inside the house. Herbert came
last, thrusting a reluctant Maudie ahead of him, and closed
the door. At the sound Miss Rudd darted back from the
stairs and stood in front of Charles Crawford.

"I told you, Harry. I told you never to set foot in my
house again with your thieving ways. Tell your friends to
go, Harry. I won't have them in my house!"

"You know her?" Miss Seton asked in a puzzled voice.

Charles Crawford looked at her savagely and blushed.
"No, I don't know her, you little dope."

He shifted his feet and tried to appear nonchalant under
Miss Rudd's unblinking stare. Miss Seton began to giggle.

Miss Rudd's eyes gleamed at her. "A pretty coat," she
said. "What a pretty coat."

As she spoke a woman appeared on the stairs. She was
holding Etienne the cat in her arms, stroking his fur. She was
tall and well-built and wore a stiff white uniform that
crackled as she moved down the steps. When she came closer
Miss Seton saw that she was quite young, not over thirty,
and heavily handsome, with dark skin and smooth dark hair
braided in a coronet around her head.

She said, "Let them alone, Frances."

Miss Rudd nodded her head back and forth.

"My dear friend, Floraine," she cried. She plucked at
Floraine's sleeve as she passed. Floraine paid no attention.

"I am Floraine Larue," she said in a brisk voice, "Miss
Rudd's companion."

Miss Seton felt a surge of relief at the sight of this com-
petent-looking nurse. She said, "We've lost our bus-driver.
He got out of the bus and came here."

"Here?" Floraine raised her thick black eyebrows. "I'm sure you're mistaken. No one came here."

"No one came here," Miss Rudd repeated, nodding her head.

"No one at all," said Floraine.

Chapter 3

FLORAINE TURNED ON A WALL SWITCH AND THE enormous crystal chandelier in the center of the hall sprang into light. It was yellowed with age and the crystals threw grotesque dangling shadows on the gilt ceiling.

"They clink," Miss Rudd said, pointing. "They clink very prettily."

"Hush, Frances." Floraine moved quickly towards a heavy oak door and it opened with a shriek of hinges. "You understand we rarely use these rooms and are not prepared for company. But there is a grate in here. I shall build a fire."

Miss Seton found her voice. "But what about the driver—and the shots?"

Charles Crawford put a warning hand on her arm. "Why not get warm first?" he said dryly, and pushed her, not gently, through the open door.

In front of the fireplace was a pile of split wood which Floraine began thrusting into the grate. Mr. Hunter offered to help her but Floraine, with a fine show of teeth, said she was quite used to work of this kind.

"Take off your wraps," she added over her shoulder, "and sit down. Will you turn on the light, Frances?"

Miss Rudd darted to the switch and a second crystal chandelier blazed in the center of the room. There were no lamps although the room was so huge that the chandelier's light did not reach the corners. On the floor were two Persian rugs faded and worn thin in spots. The furniture was chiefly brown mohair, two well-worn chesterfields with chairs to match. The chairs looked rickety and listed to one side.

What a queer room, Miss Seton thought, and wondered whether it was simply because it was so old and out-of-date and had no lamps. Then she discovered with a shock that there was no furniture at all in the corners, it had all been brought into the center of the room and grouped around the fireplace.

As if most of it had been taken away, she thought. She looked at the walls and saw two gilt-framed oil paintings, in need of cleaning, one of Montcalm, the other of Frontenac. Where other paintings had once been there were pale rectangles on the walls.

They probably had a whole set of historical paintings, Miss Seton decided. The rest have been taken away. Sold? Or destroyed by Frances Rudd?

"Nosy parker," said Mr. Crawford's voice close to her ear. "Take time off to give me your coat."

Blushing, Miss Seton hurriedly removed her coat. Mr. Crawford took it and examined the fur. He said, grinning, "Hmmm. Sable? Where have you been all my life?"

"I don't know," Miss Seton said crossly. "But I know where I'm going to be the rest of your life. Missing."

"Suits me," Crawford said with a shrug. "No harm in asking."

"This wing is not used," Floraine explained again for the benefit of the others. "There are only the two of us, you see."

"Two?" Mrs. Vista sank down on one of the mohair chesterfields and raised a fine spray of dust. "Two? I thought that Miss—Miss Budd—"

"Rudd," Floraine said.

"Miss Rudd said there were . . ."

From the hall came a cackle of laughter and a long-drawn-out sniffle.

"Miss Rudd is imaginative," Floraine said delicately.

Mrs. Vista looked out into the hall and then back at Floraine. "Imaginative," she repeated thoughtfully. "You mean she's—batty?"

"Oh, a little," Floraine said. "A very little."

She went back into the hall. Her voice came through the door, firm but pleasant:

"You promised me you wouldn't cry today, Frances."

"Oh, I can't help it," Miss Rudd moaned. "It's so sad. Everything is so sad."

"You'd better not cry any more. These people are nice, Frances, quite nice. You must go in and be pleasant to them. They are your guests, and you mustn't *pinch* any of them."

"Just the fat one."

"Not any of them," Floraine said sharply. "Be pleasant

and ask their names while I make some coffee. Do you understand, Frances?"

Miss Rudd moaned again but Floraine's brisk footsteps became fainter. They sounded as if Floraine was impatient. With Miss Rudd, Miss Seton thought, or with us?

Company would naturally be a nuisance in such a household. It would be difficult enough to manage Miss Rudd, without additional complications. But there were the two rifle shots. Indicating, Miss Seton thought dryly, a new high in impatience.

"Why do I assume Floraine did the shooting?" she murmured.

"I don't know." Joyce Hunter was beside her, gazing at her with her clear cold eyes. "Why do you?"

"Floraine was wearing white," Miss Seton said in a whisper. "I saw something white move at one of the second-floor windows right after the shots."

"Yes." Joyce bit her lower lip and stared pensively at the ceiling. It was her thinking pose. She said at last, "I think you're right. You'd have to be on the second floor to make those shots."

"And the driver—if he isn't here, where is he?"

"Where is who?" Mr. Goodwin asked absently. He was sitting at the end of the chesterfield opposite Mrs. Vista, and gazing meditatively at his hat. "Phenomenal. Phenomenal phate. Peculiar Parca. What were you saying, Miss Seton?"

Miss Seton looked at him in annoyance. "I wasn't really talking to you but I'll repeat. *Where is the bus-driver?*"

"Who knows?" said Mr. Goodwin. "We are all ephemeral. Here today. Gone tomorrow. Ephemeral effigies."

"That's excellent, Anthony," Mrs. Vista said encouragingly. "I shall have to remember it."

"Ephemeral effigies or not," Miss Seton said acidly. "Even ephemeral effigies have to disappear *to* some place . . ."

"Not necessarily," said Mrs. Vista loyally.

". . . and I want to know where. If we don't find him we'll have to stay in this house until someone finds the bus and traces us here. That might take days. If you'll kindly descend to our plane for a moment, Mr. Goodwin, you'll understand that."

"Oh, no!" Maudie cried. "Oh, no! I couldn't stay here. I'm so frightened. That *woman. Look at her!*"

All eyes turned to the door. Miss Rudd was moving soundlessly into the room with a kind of slithering motion. She skimmed over to the chesterfield, plucked Mr. Goodwin's hat from his hands and put it on over her white lace cap. Then she skimmed back to the door and closed it. The whole thing was done in ten seconds.

"Odd," Mr. Goodwin said thoughtfully.

Mrs. Vista found her bellow and used it. "Really! Anthony, your lovely hat! You shouldn't have let her take it!"

"I think it was a silly hat," Joyce said. She had given up all hope of being debauhed by Mr. Goodwin and was feeling cross. "Talk, talk, talk!" She flung herself into a chair. "Why don't we do something about something? Poppa!"

Mr. Hunter who was bending over the fire straightened up obediently. "Yes, my dear?"

"You'll have to command that nurse to produce our driver."

"C-command?"

"Certainly, command. We'll have the coffee first and then you can tell her very firmly. It will be dark soon, and I for one don't feel like staying overnight in this house."

"Besides," said Herbert from the windows, "it's snowing again."

It was also getting dark. The snow had changed and the soft feathery flakes that clung to the window looked gray, like huge particles of dust.

Paula Lashley looked out and shivered. She had not taken off her ski-suit but merely flung the hood back from her head. She sat hunched in a chair, with Chad Ross standing beside her like a nasty-tempered but faithful watchdog.

"I want to go home," Paula whispered. "Please, Chad. I can't go through with it."

Chad was silent for a time. Then he said in a hard voice, "It's what I expected. You haven't the guts of a worm, Paula."

"No—I know." She bowed her head.

"Just how are you going to get home, *now?*"

"The driver must be here," Paula said. "The nurse was lying. We could search the house."

"Very eager, aren't you?" Chad said. "Do you think we can just walk into a stranger's house and search it, like the police?"

They were talking in low whispers, but even though Charles Crawford was on the other side of the room he heard the word police. He sauntered over to Paula and Chad, keeping his hands in his pockets.

"What's this about police?" he asked casually.

"None of your business," Chad said.

"No? All right." He smiled amiably at Chad. "Anyone ever tell you you could make a fortune frightening babies?

Look into it, eh?" He turned and walked away towards Miss Gracie Morning.

Gracie was sitting comfortably and happily in front of the fire, drying out her long beautiful legs and combing out each of her auburn curls separately and with infinite care. She paid no attention to the bickering going on around her. She accepted her fate gracefully, partly because she was naturally even-tempered and partly because she was not hungry like the others, having consumed three-quarters of a pound of Laura Secord chocolates.

Crawford sat down beside her and frowned into the fire. Gracie thought he looked cute.

She said, "I'm just *crazy* about stern men."

Crawford tried to think of a suitable reply to this and eventually hit upon, "I'm crazy about auburn hair,"—which was true enough.

"So am I," Gracie said confidentially. "That's why I have it."

"Ah? So."

"Mr. Goodwin is a very peculiar man, don't you think so?"

Here again the truth seemed best. "He is," Crawford said, "rather."

Gracie rolled her eyes. "Very! But I guess we're all funny in some ways, though some of us are worse than others. Like the old lady."

"Miss Rudd? She's not so old. Fifty, perhaps."

"That's old."

"You think so?" Crawford said sadly. "I'm nearly forty."

"I'm twenty-three."

"A good age."

"But I'm much older than my years," Gracie confided.

"Yes, I can see that," Crawford said.

Gracie was not entirely satisfied with this reply, so she returned to her curl combing to think it over.

Joyce Hunter had taken off her ski-jacket and was now walking around the room examining the furnishings with a businesslike air.

"Quaint but grim," was her verdict when she returned again to Isobel Seton. "Floraine's been gone a long time. You don't suppose she's skipped out, do you?"

Her father let out a long exasperated sigh. "Why on earth should she skip out?"

Joyce thumped her feet impatiently against the floor. "Poppa, you mustn't always be asking why this and why that. I don't know why. I just *feel* things. I felt something about the bus-driver and he disappeared. Now I feel something about Floraine, and it wouldn't surprise me if she disappeared."

"I guess we'll have to burn you as a witch," Miss Seton remarked, "before you put the hex on the rest of us."

"You shouldn't joke about sinister things," Joyce said.

"No, I suppose not," Miss Seton said gloomily and strolled over to the fireplace to join Gracie and Crawford.

Gracie welcomed her brightly. "I was just telling Mr. Crawford how crazy I am about stern men."

"Are you?" said Miss Seton.

"I think Mr. Crawford is terribly stern, don't you?"

Miss Seton examined the point. "Droopy," she said, "not stern. He is no longer youthful."

"I am as youthful as possible," Crawford said coldly. "Considering the circumstances, I think I'm downright boyish."

"Oh, the circumstances aren't so bad," Gracie offered cheerfully. "Even supposing the old lady is crazy, well, I had an aunt who was a little crazy and she didn't do any harm. Kind of sad, she was."

The oak door creaked open and Floraine came back into the room with a large tray of tarnished silver containing a coffee percolator, cups and saucers, and a plate of sandwiches. The sandwiches gave off a strong fishy odor.

Floraine set the tray down on a mahogany refectory table placed against one wall, and drew up a chair beside it. She sat down and began to pour out the coffee, with a calm, self-possessed air which Miss Seton found rather disturbing.

She's not curious enough, Miss Seton thought. She hasn't asked any questions and she looks as though she doesn't intend to answer any, whether she can or not.

"Sugar?" Floraine asked her, as if she were aware of Miss Seton's thoughts.

"Please," Miss Seton said meekly. "Two lumps."

"One lump," Floraine said with a slight lift of her brows. "We're rationed and not equipped for guests."

Feeling very guilty indeed, Miss Seton settled for one lump, reached for her coffee and retired as far from Floraine as she could get. When she had settled herself in the chair beside Paula Lashley, she found she had forgotten to take a sandwich. In spite of their repellent odor, the sandwiches were food and Miss Seton had seen no food since leaving the train. She got up again and was making her way back to the table when the light in the chandelier flickered and went out.

A babble of voices rose instantly in the darkness. "Who

did that?" "Turn it on again!" "Miss Seton turned the light off."

"Oh, I did not!" Miss Seton protested feebly.

"It's quite all right." Floraine's voice was cool. "This has happened before. We have our own diesel generator and it frequently fails us. I'll ask Frances to fetch the oil lamps."

She went across the room and out into the hall and called, "Frances! Where are you, Frances? Go and bring down the oil lamps."

There was no answer but a shuffling of feet from some place in the hall. Floraine, apparently satisfied, came back into the room and took her place at the table. There was no light in the room except the fire and Floraine's face was turned away from it, but Miss Seton fancied that Floraine was smiling.

After a time Miss Rudd's voice began to whine from the doorway. "I can't find the lamps, Floraine. Someone has stolen them. I don't like the dark with Harry here."

Floraine rose again and went to the door. "You've hidden them again, Frances," she said patiently. "Where did you hide them?"

"Oh, I didn't! I didn't!"

"We'll have to remain in the dark all night unless you tell me."

Miss Rudd hid her face in the black shawl and wept. "Oh, I didn't hide them! I just put them away so these thieving friends of Harry's couldn't get them."

"Where?"

"Oh, I can't tell you, Floraine. These thieves will hear me."

"Whisper it."

Floraine bent over and Miss Rudd said in a loud sibilant whisper, "In the *cellar. Aren't* I clever?"

"Very clever." Floraine walked away down the hall. Miss Rudd remained in the doorway rubbing her face with her shawl.

"Well, Anthony," Mrs. Vista said sternly. "Hadn't you better ask her for your hat?"

"Oh, quite." Mr. Goodwin said bitterly. "Oh, yes, yes, yes."

He advanced on Miss Rudd, making amiable grimaces. "I say. That hat. Hat." He patted his head coaxingly. "Hat. Chapeau."

Miss Rudd merely stared at him as if he were crazy.

"You're going at it all wrong!" Joyce cried. "You're simply

supposed to treat her as if she were quite normal. I took a course in psychology, abnormal, subnormal and normal."

"Use them all," Charles Crawford said dryly.

"*This* is how you do it." Joyce walked over to Miss Rudd, smiling brightly. "Hello," she said. "I'm Joyce Hunter. This is Mr. Goodwin."

Miss Rudd bowed politely. "How do you do, Mr. Goodwin, you vicious son of a bitch."

Mr. Goodwin gulped. "How—how do you do."

"Mr. Goodwin wants his hat," Joyce continued, undaunted. "We expect to be leaving soon, but Mr. Goodwin cannot go without his hat."

"He will freeze," said Miss Rudd.

Joyce nodded encouragingly. "Of course he will. Perhaps if you give him back his hat Mr. Goodwin will give you his tie which is much prettier."

"No, thank you kindly," Miss Rudd replied in a reasonable tone.

A faint light appeared in the hall and Floraine came in carrying two oil lamps and set them on the mantel. She said over her shoulder, "Please don't annoy Miss Rudd. She doesn't like strangers to come too close to her."

"My hat," Mr. Goodwin bleated.

"I'll get it for you." She went out and came back in a minute carrying a few strips of green felt. "I'm afraid it won't be much use to you any more. Miss Rudd loves to cut things. She will apologize, won't you, Frances? Say you're sorry, Frances."

"I'm sorry," Miss Rudd said brightly.

So the first round was Miss Rudd's, Isobel Seton reflected as she sipped the last of her coffee.

The room was becoming very hot and steamy and smelled of wet clothes and salmon sandwiches and Gracie Morning's primeval perfume. Miss Seton's eyelids felt heavy, so she leaned her head against the back of the chair, too inert to force the issue of the disappearing bus-driver and the rifle shots. The more she considered them, the more preposterous and unreal they seemed, especially now that Miss Rudd had been sent up to her room and Floraine was talking pleasantly to Charles Crawford in front of the fire. She wasn't in the least sinister, but a normal attractive young woman.

Miss Seton dozed for a while and dreamed of an encounter with Miss Rudd, who, armed with a garden shears, hacked expertly at Miss Seton's sable coat.

When she awoke the scene was much the same as it had

been, except that the blinds were drawn over the windows
and Floraine's voice was sharper as she talked.

"We are not inhospitable," she was saying. "We are simply
unable to accommodate you. The Chateau is only a few miles
further along the road . . ."

"A few miles," Crawford repeated. "We couldn't get half a
mile under the circumstances."

"You understand, Miss Rudd and I are alone here. We
have no extra bedding or food, nor fuel to heat the extra
rooms. We have no telephone. We are completely isolated."

"Why?"

"Why?" She stared at him. Miss Seton, watching her, had
the impression that Floraine was deliberately exaggerating
the expressions of her face and voice in order that the other
people in the room should not miss them.

She's talking to all of us, Miss Seton thought.

"Why?" Floraine said again. "You realize Miss Rudd's condition. Her family do not want her in a sanitarium. Miss
Rudd herself prefers to stay here. It is her home."

"Must be a dull life for you," Crawford said.

Floraine let out a slight laugh. "Oh, no. I don't care for
excitement and I am paid well. And besides, my fiancé has
gone to war."

"We're willing to pay you for a night's lodging."

"No, I couldn't . . ."

"We'll pay very well. You realize that we have to stay
here anyway. You can't kick us out. Let's arrange it without too much unpleasantness."

Floraine's eyes glistened. "How much?"

"Ritz rates. Five dollars a head, and a bonus if you cough
up the bus-driver and no questions asked."

"Questions?"

"He may have had his reasons for skipping. We guarantee
to let that pass if he deposits us at the lodge tomorrow
morning. We'll back up his story about a breakdown."

"But how absurd!" Floraine cried. "You're bargaining
with me about a man I've never seen or heard of in my
life! A bus-driver! Surely if such a man came here Miss Rudd
would tell you, even if I wanted to keep it a secret. People
like Miss Rudd tell everything."

"She may not have seen him," Crawford said. "He may
be here in this house without your having seen him either.
It's a big place."

"Ridiculous!"

"All right," Crawford said easily. "Forget him. The most
vital question is bed. Fifty-five dollars."

"And breakfast?"

"Fifty cents apiece," Crawford said grimly.

"Sixty dollars and fifty cents," Floraine said. "Very well." She held out her hand.

"That woman will go far," Miss Seton murmured, reaching for her purse and extracting some bills. "By the time her young man comes back she'll have a dowry that looks like the Chase National Bank."

They all paid willingly enough, except Gracie Morning, who said there wasn't a bed in the world worth five bucks and that anybody who paid in advance for anything was a sucker. In the interests of peace Miss Seton hastily fished out another bill, and Floraine, accompanied by Herbert as a volunteer, went out to fetch more lamps.

Waiting for them to return, Miss Seton curled up in her chair and studied Mr. Goodwin with half-closed eyes. Contrary to the magazine report, Mr. Goodwin had shown no signs of relapsing into a drunken stupor.

It was an unfortunate moment to examine Mr. Goodwin, for he was giving birth to a sonnet and his face was moving rhythmically and unbeautifully in labor. He looked quite incapable of debauchery.

"Englishmen are not great lovers," Miss Seton murmured with the false air of a connoisseur.

Mr. Hunter who had been watching her for some time let out a gasp of surprise. "No. No, I daresay they're not."

He looked around to see if Joyce was still asleep, and finding that she was he stroked his mustache knowingly and remarked that it had something to do with glands.

"What has?" Miss Seton asked.

"The—the—what you said."

"Oh. Too many or too few?"

"Too few or too many what?"

"Glands."

"Oh."

"Well?"

Mr. Hunter flushed. "I don't believe it has anything to do with number."

"Intensity, perhaps?"

"I don't know," he said irritably. "I think you're just *doing* this."

"Doing what?" Miss Seton asked in surprise.

"There. You did it again. 'Doing what?' I'm sure *I* didn't start this conversation."

"I'm equally sure I didn't."

"You spoke."

"To myself only," "Miss Seton said sternly. "You horned in."

"Merely out of politeness."

"Politeness? Ha!" said Miss Seton.

With a final snort Mr. Hunter rose to his feet and approached Mr. Goodwin.

"I understand," he said, "that we'll have to double up in the rooms because there isn't enough bedding. I'd be glad to share a room with you."

"Share?" Mr. Goodwin's features became ominously still. "Did you say *share* a room?"

"Anthony dear," said Mrs. Vista with an edge in her voice, "it will be just for one night. I'm sure you'll find Mr. Hunter a delightful person . . ."

"He will not," said Mr. Hunter decisively. "I presume he wants to have a room to himself while the rest of us herd like cattle."

"I wonder," Mrs. Vista meditated aloud, "whom *I* shall choose. Let me see. Someone *thin,* and preferably *quiet.* That girl in the corner over there. What's your name, my dear?"

Paula smiled slightly and said, "Paula Lashley."

"That man isn't your husband, is he?"

"No," Paula said, while Chad growled something unintelligible.

"Well, that's settled," Mrs. Vista said. "What about the rest of you?"

It was decided that Isobel Seton and Gracie were to share one room, and the Thropples another. Since Joyce was still sleeping on the chesterfield and no one particularly wanted her as a bedfellow, she was allotted a bedroom to herself.

"A small one," Mrs. Vista decided, always fair, "and perhaps the scrummiest."

Goodwin announced that he would stay downstairs on the chesterfield and keep the fire lit for warmth, since he practically never slept anyway. Crawford yawned and said he'd take anyone who had a good loud snore and didn't mind competition.

"I never snore," Mr. Hunter said hastily.

"Then you take the young man over there who growls," Mrs. Vista said, "and Mr. Crawford can have a room to himself, if there is one."

"Thanks," Crawford said. "And if there isn't one?"

"Oh, don't be a pessimist," Mrs. Vista said easily.

She raised herself from the chesterfield, and creaked and waddled to the door. In the hall Floraine and Herbert Thropple had appeared with several lamps. Mrs. Vista explained the sleeping arrangements to Floraine and Floraine agreed that they seemed the best possible.

She led the way upstairs. The others filed out into the hall and followed her, while the house groaned under the whip of the rising wind.

Chapter 4

JOYCE, PROPELLED INTO THE HALL BY HER father, stopped at the bottom of the stairs and said she had no intention of going to bed yet. It was only nine o'clock, she had just had a sleep and she felt like staying up to talk to Mr. Goodwin.

"Absolutely no," said Mr. Hunter.

"Oh, don't be such a heavy," Joyce said. "I've never really talked to a poet and I'm nineteen and I don't think you should begrudge your own daughter her chances."

"Chances to do what?" said Mr. Hunter with a sinister look.

"Oh, Poppa! Your generation is so one-track. I mean, there *are* things besides sex." She reached up and kissed his cheek. "Have a good sleep, silly."

Mr. Hunter escorted her back to the sitting room. Goodwin was pacing up and down the room.

"Hello," Joyce said brightly. "Mind if I come in?"

"I am composing," said Mr. Goodwin.

"Oh, that's all right. You won't disturb me. Good night, Poppa."

"Good night," Mr. Hunter said coldly. "And see here, Goodwin, none of your funny work."

It was a strong manly exit, and Mr. Hunter, feeling very set up, joined the others on the second floor.

The rooms had already been allotted. There were eight bedrooms on this floor, Floraine explained, and of course the third floor had been shut off for years. The eight bedrooms opened on the hall in pairs, a simple mathematical arrangement which fitted in with the way the house had looked from the outside.

There was one bathroom, Floraine added. It was at the end

of the hall beside the staircase that led to the third floor. There might be enough water for three people to take baths and if the water should be a rather peculiar color no one was to worry. The pipes were rusted, that was all. On the other hand if anyone turned on the hot water and no water emerged it meant that the pipes were frozen as well as rusted . . .

"Pleasant dreams!" Floraine said with a sweet smile, and flitted off down the back stairs, holding the lamp above her head.

Isobel Seton stood in the doorway of the room she was to share with Gracie and stared thoughtfully at Floraine's disappearing back.

"There's a woman," she said, "that I could find it very easy to dislike."

Gracie agreed. "Come on in and let's get that door locked."

Isobel came inside and closed the door. "There's a lock but no key."

"We can use the furniture." Gracie stood in the middle of the room and surveyed it. In its heyday it might have been sumptuous, but the heavy rose damask drapes were grayed with dust and age, and the huge mahogany bed was cracked along the headboard. Here, too, there were indications that various pieces of furniture had been removed from the room—marks beside the grate where a heavy chair had once been, rectangular spaces on the wallpaper less faded than the rest. The rug, too, had been taken away and cold air skimmed across the bare floor.

"Hellish little nook," Gracie said cheerfully.

Isobel sat down on the edge of the bed with her coat draped over her shoulders and shivered. "Don't look now but did somebody forget to put panes in those windows?"

Gracie pushed aside the damask drapes. "There are panes. And look—a radiator! But it's cold."

"Probably frozen," Isobel said grimly. "Aren't we going to be cosy under our two blankets! I'm beginning to think we should have stayed in that bus, wolves or no wolves."

"Funny," Gracie said pensively. "At the time this seemed the only thing to do. I mean, it was so logical."

"Exactly."

"It sort of looks as though we were taken in. Somebody did some dirty work."

"But why?"

"Oh, nuts," Gracie said in a different tone. "We're just tired. I don't want to stick my oar in. If there's a mystery I want to keep it a mystery. The only thing to do in a place like this is to get inside a room with somebody you

can trust, put the furniture in front of the door and be prepared to yell like hell."

She came over to the bed and began unfolding the sheets
and the two motheaten blankets.

"Let's figure it out," Isobel said. "We must have stayed in
the bus about half an hour after the driver left. We walked
approximately half an hour. Miss Rudd delayed us at the
door about fifteen minutes. That's an hour and a quarter.
The driver obviously knew where he was going, he couldn't
have taken a chance on finding a house in this part of the
country. So, if he knew the route and wasn't stopped by
rifle shots, he probably covered the ground in fifteen minutes. Subtract that from our hour and a quarter and you
have one hour to disappear."

"I don't believe he disappeared," Gracie said. "He's here,
all right. Maybe he and Floraine will arrange something . . ."

"If he's here," Isobel said calmly, "let's find him."

"You *are* nuts," Gracie said. "If he doesn't want to be
found I'm not the girl to go looking for him."

"Do you remember what he looked like?"

Gracie had lost interest in bed-making and had picked
up Isobel's hat and was trying it on in front of the bureau
mirror.

"This is sort of cute on me," she said with open admiration.
"But then I can wear anything."

"That's nice," Isobel said absently. "I think he was big,
wasn't he?"

"Who?"

"The bus-driver. Big, and with a gray overcoat and a
visored gray cap and pimples at the back of his neck. It's
his face I'm worried about."

"Let him worry about his own face," Gracie said cheerfully. "I'm going to bed. Move off there, will you?"

Isobel stood up and stared at her witheringly. "Do you
mean to say you haven't the nerve to search the house?"

"You guessed it," Gracie said. "And neither have you."

"Nonsense. Of course I have. I just thought it would be
better if two of us . . ."

"Not me. Get one of the men to go with you."

"Men! I never saw such a bunch of ineffectual hag-
ridden pipsqueaks . . ."

"You haven't been around enough," Gracie said. "Now,
take me. Maybe I haven't been to so many places as you but
I sure have covered the ground thoroughly. And what I
learned is this: never expect anything from any of them but
pretend you do. That's my system."

"I have no doubt it's an excellent one," Isobel said coldly. "Meanwhile you'd better get into bed. *I'm* taking the lamp."

"And leave me here in the dark!" Gracie squealed. "You leave that lamp here!"

"You little coward," Isobel said, and walked firmly towards the door with the lamp in her hands.

She stepped out into the hall and closed the door behind her. There was no light coming from beneath the next door, which was Floraine's. Isobel moved slowly past it.

Miss Rudd's room came next. Though Miss Rudd had been sent to bed an hour ago her lamp was still lit. Then three things happened almost simultaneously. The doorknob of Miss Rudd's room began to move, something brushed against Isobel's ankles, and in a split second Isobel turned down the wick of her lamp.

She began to creep backwards towards her own door. The darkness had a strange quality of being alive. It was not absence of light but something more real, a kind of black clammy air which seeped in through the walls and the doors, a dark fog rising from the cellar.

No one came out of Miss Rudd's room. Isobel stood with the unlit lamp in her hand and something moving in the darkness at her feet. She fumbled in the pocket of her dress and found a match and struck it against the wall. The light flared.

Standing at her feet, motionless, was a large amiable white rat. He looked intelligently at Isobel, far more intelligently than she looked at him. Apparently satisfied with her, he gave a good-natured twitch of his whiskers and scampered off down the hall.

Isobel let the match fall and opened the door of her room.

"What is it?" Gracie's voice came urgently from the bed. "Now what?"

"A rat," Isobel said, swallowing hard.

"A rat? Well, what did you expect?"

"Not," Isobel said shakily, "an ordinary rat. He was quite —quite blasé."

"Well, light that lamp and crawl into bed and stay there, if you're going to be scared skinny by a poor little rat."

The lamp was lit again. Gracie sat up in bed with a blanket over her shoulders. "I remembered something for you. There was a name-card above the mirror in the bus. It had M. Hearst printed on it."

"Hush," Isobel said. She had her head bent towards the door. In the hall someone was calling in a husky penetrating whisper:

"Suzanne! Suzanne, where are you? Oh, dear, oh, dear!"

"I rather hoped," Isobel said in a cracked voice, "I rather hoped Miss Rudd would be sleeping."

The plaintive whispers went on. "Oh, Suzanne! Oh, you naughty girl! Come, you vixen!"

Then Floraine's voice, steady but a little impatient: "Frances, give me those scissors."

"I haven't got any scissors, my dear friend. You told me not to take the scissors and I wouldn't. You know I wouldn't, Floraine!"

"You have them hidden under your shawl."

There was a brief scuffle and a cry of surprise from Miss Rudd.

"Why, there they are! Under my shawl! Someone must have put them there, Floraine. That thin one with the sharp nose."

"Oh, be quiet, Frances," Floraine said wearily. "Come back into your room and I'll tell you a story."

And the house became quiet again except for the creaking of the walls as the wind pressed against them.

Subdued and silent, Isobel set the lamp on the bureau and turned the wick low. Then she lay down on the bed, covering her eyes with one arm. She stayed awake for some time listening to the strange medley of sounds, the howling of the wind, Gracie's quiet even breathing, the sudden banging of the steam radiator, the sharp quick tap of sleet against the windows, for the snow was fine again with the rising of the wind.

It's so noisy, she thought. We couldn't even hear danger if it should approach. Someone could come along that balcony outside the windows and step right in . . .

"Gracie," she whispered. But Gracie was sleeping and finally Isobel slept too for a time.

When she awoke she heard a new sound in the room, a buzzing like a swarm of bees, a steady purring like many giant cats ready to maul their kill.

She kept her eyes closed tightly. It couldn't be bees, of course. And there was only one cat, Etienne, and he couldn't be—he couldn't possibly be . . .

But he was. Isobel moved her hand a little and there he was stretched out beside her on the bed, his eyes glowing. So close to her, he looked huge and savage as a tiger.

"Scram," she said. Etienne blinked and began to wave his tail.

Gracie stirred and said, "Leave me alone."

"Wake up, Gracie. Wake up. We have company."

Gracie yawned and sat up. When she saw the cat she lay down again quickly and said, "My God. Is this a zoo?"

"Gracie, tell him to go away."

"Tell him yourself."

"Push him, then," Isobel said.

"Push him yourself," Gracie said. "How did he get in? Did you bring him in with you?"

"Oh, don't be silly."

Etienne appeared to be following the conversation with some interest.

"Well, how did he get in?" Gracie said. "And why?"

"A refugee from Miss Rudd," Isobel said. "A very reasonable animal."

"Not reasonable enough to turn doorknobs," Gracie pointed out. "Somebody must have let him in."

"Go away, Etienne," Isobel said. *"Allez-vous-en!* Scram!"

The cat leaped silently to the floor and stalked away. Isobel hurriedly opened the door and let him out into the hall. She came back to the bed, looking worried.

"Miss Rudd," she said slowly, "had a pair of scissors and she just loves to cut things. First, Mr. Goodwin's hat."

"Maybe she's working up by degrees," Gracie said. "Hat, rat, cat, and then us."

There was a silence. Then Isobel said, "I don't think I'm going to sleep."

"Well, I *am*. Go down and talk to Goodie."

"You wouldn't mind?"

"I'm too tired to mind anything," Gracie said sleepily. "Give my love to Goodie."

Mr. Goodwin, however, was in no position to accept it. He had fallen asleep in front of the fire. His mouth was open and he was making unlovely sounds.

Isobel stared at him bitterly, but the perfidious Mr. Goodwin did not stir. She sat down in a chair holding the lamp like a wrathful virgin arrived too late.

Perhaps Mr. Goodwin would wake up. Even if he didn't, it was warmer down here and there was no balcony outside the windows, and you could watch the door.

She watched the door until her eyes grew heavy. Mr. Goodwin did not wake up and nothing came through the door. She set the lamp on the floor and leaned back and closed her eyes, only to open them again quickly at the sound of footsteps.

Joyce Hunter was standing in the doorway. She had a small flashlight in her hand which she clicked off as soon as she saw Isobel.

"Well," she said in a whisper. "What are you doing down here, Miss Seton?"

"Sitting," Isobel said, rather unnecessarily. "I couldn't sleep. So I came down hoping Mr. Goodwin would be awake. But he isn't."

"Not so loud," Joyce said, frowning. She closed the door. She continued to speak in low, sinister whispers. "There's something funny about this house."

"You don't mean to tell me," Isobel said dryly. "And to think I was just on the verge of buying it for a cosy little country home."

Joyce ignored this. "They have scads of food, for one thing, and all they gave us was those salmon sandwiches. And Floraine said they hadn't much fuel, but the coal bin is stocked to the brim . . ."

"You were down in the cellar?"

"Naturally," Joyce said. "I couldn't sit around and watch Mr. Goodwin sleep."

Isobel stared at her suspiciously. "Do you always carry around flashlights?"

"No, I stole this one from Mr. Crawford's overcoat pocket," Joyce said modestly. "I thought it would be a good idea to find the bus-driver."

"And I suppose you did?" Isobel said with heavy irony.

Joyce looked at her thoughtfully. "Not *exactly*."

"What do you mean?"

"Come on down cellar and see for yourself." She put her hand on the doorknob, then removed it and said curtly, "I suppose I can trust you, can I?"

"As much as I can trust you," Isobel said, annoyed.

Joyce turned on the flashlight and opened the door.

The hall seemed interminably long. On either side the doors were shut, and, as she passed each one, Isobel thought, he may be in there. Or there. Or this one. He may be watching us.

Joyce turned the flashlight briefly on the last door and put her hand on the knob.

"This is the kitchen," she whispered. "You go down to the cellar from here."

Isobel followed her into the room pausing a moment to look behind her. Then she closed the door silently and followed Joyce down the steps to the cellar. A queer pungent odor came up at her, the smell of whitewash and rancid food, and damp cement.

"Nothing in this room," Joyce said, "but a bag of rotting

potatoes and a couple of trunks. The trunks—" she added pointedly—"are both empty."

She was fumbling with the latch of a heavy door reinforced with bars of iron. There was a padlock on the door but it hadn't been locked.

They stepped into the next room. It was smaller and the air was warmer and quite dry. To the left was the furnace and beside it the coal bin well-stocked with coal.

"Here," Joyce said, "take the light and hold it over here."

Isobel kept the light fixed on the coal bin. Joyce picked up a poker and began to prod the coal. Finally she bent over and picked something from the floor. Then she held out her hand to Isobel and in the palm of it lay a metal monogram covered with soot.

"M.H.," Isobel said slowly, remembering the name-plate in the bus, M. Hearst.

"Hold it," Joyce said. "I found it and hid it again."

Isobel took the monogram in her hand and stared at it. Joyce began prodding in the coal again. When she straightened up she had something else, a black button and a narrow band of leather.

"His hat band," she said in a grim voice. "And a button from his coat. The monogram was on his hat band."

Isobel turned away with a shudder and fixed her eyes on the furnace.

"Where's the rest of him?" she said in a hushed voice.

In the faint light Joyce's face looked pale and very childish. She's scared, Isobel thought fleetingly. All her words and actions are just putting up a front.

"I don't know." Joyce bit her lip and seemed suddenly ready to cry. "They—couldn't have put him in the furnace?"

Because Isobel herself had been thinking of the same possibility, she spoke rather sharply. "No, of course not! Don't be silly. We have no reason to think he was—he was murdered."

Joyce looked silently down at the hat band she was holding.

"I mean, it's so silly," Isobel added desperately. "He wouldn't have gotten out of the bus and come here just to be murdered. It's insane."

"So," Joyce said, "is Miss Rudd."

They looked at each other, then Isobel dropped her eyes and turned away. "I'm going to look around a little bit. There's a workbench over there, you can sit on it and wait for me. I might find something—something reassuring."

Or damning, she added to herself.

But, except for the hat band and the monogram and the button, the cellar seemed an average one. There were pieces of broken furniture along one wall, a work table with a few simple tools, a disemboweled couch and a shelf containing paints and brushes. From the shelf she picked up a can and turned the light on it.

"What's that?" Joyce asked.

"Ski-wax," Isobel said. "A fresh can of it."

"That's funny. You wouldn't expect Miss Rudd to ski and Floraine couldn't very well leave her alone."

"Besides," Isobel said, "there are no skis. Come over and hold the light, will you?"

Joyce held the flashlight while Isobel examined the shelf and took the lid off the can of ski-wax.

"It's been used once or twice," Isobel said. "And look at the shelf. It's dusty but there isn't a spot of dust on the can. It must have been put here very recently."

Holding the can she turned decisively towards the door.

"Come on. I'm going upstairs and demand an explanation from Floraine."

"We can't demand anything," Joyce said. "It's her house, we haven't a right . . ."

"She shot at us with a rifle. That's right enough for me! Are you coming?"

It was Isobel who led the way and Joyce who trailed behind. When they reached the first floor Joyce said that whatever demanding had to be done would be done by Miss Isobel Seton alone and unaided.

"I've had enough for tonight," she said with a wan smile. "Get Gracie to go with you. You may take the flashlight and I'll stay down here with Mr. Goodwin."

So Isobel, armed with a flashlight, a button, a hat band and a monogram, went upstairs to enlist Gracie's aid.

She opened the door of the room and stopped short.

Gracie moved restlessly under the covers and muttered that she felt cold.

Isobel said nothing.

"The blankets seem so damp," Gracie complained. "Probably the roof leaks."

"No," Isobel said in a faint voice. "It's the cat."

"The cat?" Gracie opened her eyes.

"The cat." Isobel gulped. "Dead."

"Oh, you must be dreaming." Gracie paused. "You *are* dreaming, aren't you?"

"Don't be fatuous," Isobel said. "Look for yourself."

So Gracie raised herself on one elbow and saw Etienne lying with his soft throat slit and his blood soaking into the blankets.

Chapter 5

WHEN GRACIE SCREAMED THE WHOLE HOUSE sprang into action, as if it had been waiting for something to happen and was ready, holding its breath.

Bedroom doors began to open and people spilled out into the hall, clutching lamps and coats and blankets. They herded together, disheveled and frightened, asking almost in one voice: "What is it? What's happened?"

Then Gracie herself tottered out into the hall. She was fully clothed except for her shoes, and her stockings were stained dark red at the feet.

Charles Crawford pointed at the stain, and there was an instant's hush before Maudie began to scream. "Look! Herbert, I'm going to faint. I'm—going—to . . ."

So Maudie, who had been on the verge of fainting for twenty years, finally accomplished it and was bundled back into the bedroom by Herbert. Paula Lashley went with him to give Maudie first aid.

Crawford came over and took Gracie's arm. "What happened?"

"That cat," Gracie said through her teeth. "Miss Rudd killed it *on my bed*. Will somebody help me get these damned stockings off?"

Nobody offered. So Gracie, balancing herself by clinging to Crawford's arm, got the stockings off, rolled them into a ball and tossed them back into the bedroom.

Crawford looked inquiringly at Isobel.

"It's true," Isobel said sharply. "Go in and look."

"Tut, tut, tut, tut," said Mr. Hunter stroking his mustache. He caught Isobel Seton's scornful eye on him and wished there was something he could do, something positive, or heroic. But after all you can't wake a fellow at eleven o'clock at night and expect him to be a hero about a dead cat.

Chad Ross was scowling at Gracie. "You think the old lady killed it?"

"Who *else?*" Gracie said in exasperation. "My feet are cold."

Mrs. Vista mysteriously produced an enormous pair of fur mittens. "Here, put these on. I shall have to go down and break the news to Anthony. He is extremely sensitive."

At that moment Miss Rudd's door opened and she darted out into the hall. She was wearing a large gray flannel nightgown which was only partly buttoned and showed her black dress underneath. She seemed very cheerful and sang out:

"Good morning. Good morning. Good morning."

"Good morning," Crawford said hastily. "Where's Floraine?"

Instead of answering Miss Rudd threw back her head and began to bellow, "Floraine! Floraine!"

Floraine's door opened. "Stop that noise, Frances." She came out into the hall, her eyebrows raised at the gathering. She wore a well-tailored wool bathrobe and her hair hung in two braids. She looked like an older and more sinister Pocahontas.

"What is it?" she said. "Go back into your room, Frances."

Miss Rudd gazed at her mulishly.

Floraine grasped her arm and tried to push. "Go into your room!"

". . . you, you tart, you whore, you Jezebel . . ."

Floraine slapped her across the face. Isobel opened her mouth to protest, but before she could speak Miss Rudd shambled off down the hall, holding her hand to her face, and moaning.

"What's happened?" Floraine said brusquely, paying no more attention to Miss Rudd.

Crawford said, "Etienne's throat has been cut. He was found on Miss Morning's bed."

Floraine stood with her hands folded in front of her, her black eyes impassive though her voice was full of surprise. "Etienne? But that's impossible."

She went into the bedroom. When she came back she was paler and worried-looking. "But she was very fond of Etienne. I can't understand it. And I hid the scissors from her. I put them in my desk and locked the drawer."

"Maybe he committed suicide," Isobel said.

Floraine stiffened. "Frances has never raised her hand against a living thing. If she has done this it is because you've upset her. Mr. Crawford here has particularly upset her. He bears some resemblance to Miss Rudd's younger brother, Harry. So I must ask you to go back into your rooms, *all of you,* and stay there for the night. Directly after breakfast I expect you to leave."

She went back into the bedroom, and when she came out again she was holding Etienne, now a bulky parcel of gray wool, under her arm. She walked toward the head of the stairs. Finding she had no light she unceremoniously took the one Crawford was carrying and made her way downstairs. Crawford grimaced, but Isobel noticed he didn't do any objecting.

She made a quick decision and started down the steps after Floraine.

"May I come too?"

Floraine paused and turned around at the bottom of the steps. "Why?"

"Because," Isobel said clearly, "I want to talk to you. What are you going to do with the cat?"

She too had reached the bottom of the stairs and the two women stood gazing at each other. They were the same height, both tall, but Floraine was heavier.

"I'm going to put him in the furnace," Floraine said, spacing her words evenly. "If you'd care to come and watch . . ."

"I wouldn't put him in the furnace, if I were you."

"Why not?"

"It seems so unnecessary, and—and cruel."

"Cruel? He's dead, isn't he?"

Isobel felt the blood rushing to her face. "Couldn't you put him out in the snow and then bury him afterwards? After all, he was her cat and she must have—loved him once."

"I liked him too," Floraine said levelly. "I don't like sentimentality. Do you still persist in coming with me?"

"No," Isobel said. "I'll wait here for you."

"You still want to talk? Very well. I'll be back shortly."

Isobel sat on the bottom step. She found that her limbs were shaking. I'm letting it get me, she told herself. It isn't just the cat, it's everything. She could have put the driver in the furnace too—if she cut him up first . . .

She let out a little giggle, then quickly put her hand up to her mouth to stop it. Here she was, Isobel Seton, thirty-five years old, who had never done anything more exciting than attend first-nights—here she was, sitting on a step waiting for a woman to come and tell her what else had gone into that furnace besides a cat, waiting to hear about a man called M. Hearst who had entered a house and vanished in an hour.

Floraine came back, cool and unperturbed. The gray parcel was gone.

"You wanted to see me?" she said. "Come up into my room."

"No, thanks. I think my room would be just as convenient," Isobel said.

"That's all right."

Floraine led the way upstairs. Gracie Morning was not in the room, having been pressed into service for the fainting Maudie.

"Sit down," Isobel said to Floraine. "I have something to show you."

She picked up the articles Joyce had found in the cellar and thrust them in front of Floraine.

Floraine blinked. "What on earth is that? You're being very mysterious, Miss Seton. And before we go any further may I remind you that I'm not reponsible for what happens to you or the rest of them? I'm responsible for Frances Rudd."

"Don't change the subject."

"I didn't know there *was* a subject," Floraine said dryly. "You're showing me some junk . . ."

"The junk belongs to the bus-driver."

"Oh, really!" Floraine shrugged impatiently and made a move towards the door.

"I'm not through," Isobel said sharply. "So far you've been able to deny everything. You say you saw no driver, we have to believe you, temporarily. But what about those rifle shots?"

"What about them?"

"Is it the usual thing in this part of the country to shoot at strangers?"

"No . . ." Floraine said softly.

"You wouldn't give Miss Rudd a rifle to play with. I presume the rifle was yours."

"Quite right."

"And you did the shooting."

"Right again. But I wasn't shooting at strangers. I thought I was shooting at Harry, Miss Rudd's younger brother."

"Even that," Isobel said grimly, "is unusual enough. You nearly killed Mr. Goodwin."

Floraine laughed. "But I didn't kill anyone, and I have a license for the gun and you were trespassing on private property. As far as I can see I don't need to give you any explanation. But if it's really worrying you, I have warned Harry off a number of times in the same way. He's a persistent creature and Miss Rudd is afraid of him and I can't have him here. He has been trying to put her in an institution. You mustn't think that because Frances is a little peculiar she doesn't know what's going on. In some ways she's very shrewd."

"Who pays your salary?" Isobel asked.

Floraine frowned and said, "Really, you're getting into things that have no concern . . ."

"Someone must manage Miss Rudd's money."

"I do, if that's any of your business. I am Frances' cousin, and I have the power of attorney for her affairs. I am fond of Frances. She wasn't always the way she is now."

Isobel fingered the monogram M.H. After a time she said, "I'm going to keep this as a souvenir of one of the best liars I've ever seen."

Floraine smiled and said, "You're very tired. I'm sure you'll see things differently after you've had a good rest."

She spoke very convincingly, and for an instant Isobel felt that she must have imagined the whole thing. Then her eyes fell on the can of ski-wax.

"What about the ski-wax?" she said.

"Where did you get that?"

"In the cellar."

"Your prying is very thorough," Floraine said stiffly. "The wax belongs to Harry. He left it here some time ago. I put the can in the cellar yesterday morning because Frances thought it was something to eat. She ate some of it so I hid it from her."

She can explain anything, Isobel thought desperately.

Floraine said from the doorway. "Is there anything else I can relieve your mind about?"

Isobel looked up and met the impassive black eyes. "No," she said wearily. "No, thank you."

"Well, good night." She went into the hall again. Miss Rudd had come out of her room and was waiting for her.

"I thought I told you to stay in your room, Frances."

"Oh, I can't sleep with Harry in the house! You tell him to go, Floraine. You tell him he can't steal any more of my . . ."

"*Go into your room,*" Floraine said harshly. "I'm going to lock you in."

"No! Oh, no! Oh, don't lock me in!" The voice faded, and there was the bang of a door and the clicking of a lock.

Some time later Gracie came back and crawled into bed,

still wearing Mrs. Vista's fur mittens on her feet. Isobel was too depressed to move. She sat in a chair beside the windows, huddled inside her coat.

I don't believe a word Floraine said, she thought, except what Miss Rudd confirmed, that there *is* someone called Harry and that he looks something like Charles Crawford.

She took a pack of cigarettes out of her pocket and lit one. The radiator began to bang again and she thought of Etienne in the cellar burning . . .

She got up and tossed the cigarette away and stepped on it. I've got to *talk* to somebody, she thought. I can't sit here and think about that damn cat and the bus-driver.

She flung her coat over her shoulders again, reassured herself that Gracie was sleeping, and picked up the lamp.

In the hall she stopped a minute before Miss Rudd's door and tried the knob. Floraine had kept her word and Miss Rudd was locked in for the night and the light was out. She stood, listening to know if Miss Rudd had gone to sleep. Then she heard a faint muffled whispering from the room and bent her ear to the keyhole.

But it was not Miss Rudd talking there in the dark room. Even when she whispered Floraine could not conceal the nasal accent that identified her.

". . . be all right. Don't lose your nerve. She'll be gone in the morning."

There was a faint murmur in reply.

"She can't do a thing," Floraine said. "Nobody can do a thing to spoil it."

The murmur again, obviously protesting. Then a movement of feet inside the room.

Isobel walked away on tiptoe and made for Mr. Crawford's room. She had her hand up ready to knock when Joyce appeared beside her, materializing out of the darkness.

"What are you doing?" Joyce said in a low voice. "You'd better go back to your room. You don't want to stir up trouble."

Isobel said, "I *can't* stay in that room. I want somebody to talk to."

"You heard what Floraine said about Miss Rudd," Joyce hissed. "Do you want us all to be murdered?"

"I can't . . ."

"Don't be a baby! And *don't*—" Joyce narrowed her eyes— "*don't* rely on Mr. Crawford." She turned on her heel and went back to her room. Isobel noticed that she had taken off her shoes and moved silently as a cat.

What a queer girl, Isobel thought. But there had been something very convincing in her voice and Isobel went reluctantly back to her room.

She put a chair underneath the doorknob, and taking off her coat, she lay down beside Gracie. Her head ached and her cheeks burned from the wind and whenever she closed her eyes images dangled in her mind. The cat bleeding on the blanket. Miss Rudd holding the cheek Floraine had slapped. The cat again, wrapped in the gray blanket and tucked under Floraine's arm.

"She'll be gone in the morning," Floraine had said. Who was 'she'? What could she do to spoil anything for Floraine and the person with the murmur?

She couldn't have meant me, Isobel thought. I can't do anything except ask questions.

But perhaps that was what she meant. Perhaps she was really disturbed by one of the questions, if not all of them.

Gracie gave a little snore and turned on her other side, dragging the blanket with her. Isobel tugged at the blanket until she regained half of it and settled down again to think. But the images kept coming too fast and gradually they distorted beyond recognition and Isobel slept.

In a room across the hall, Mrs. Vista lay on the bed, a mountain of blankets twitching with an incipient volcano. She occupied exactly two-thirds of the bed—she had measured the amount scrupulously—but even this did not seem to be enough now that she had had a short nap.

She flapped around for a while like a walrus on ice, then she sat straight up and looked over at Paula Lashley to see if she was sleeping.

Paula's eyes were closed and she lay very quietly.

"Are you sleeping?" said Mrs. Vista loudly.

No answer.

Ah, youth, youth, thought Mrs. Vista with sadness. No nerves, no indigestion, not even any feelings, when you come to think of it.

"At any rate, I have *lived*," Mrs. Vista murmured, and thought of Cecil, the supplier of her name and fortune, and purveyor of virility.

Mrs. Vista, then Evaline Smith of Cincinnati, had gone to Europe on an organized tour. She didn't return for fifteen years and then she had defied tradition by not creeping back like a wounded animal but arriving by Clipper swaddled in mink, diamonds and smiles. She threw herself into culture. At a meeting of her Poetry Club she met Mr.

Anthony Goodwin and because he was English and alone and defenseless among Americans who misunderstood him and printed shocking lies about him in the papers, Mrs. Vista took him up. Cecil had, unaccountably, heard of this new interest, for he sent her a friendly cable telling her to watch her step or he'd send the King's Proctor after her and how was she, anyway?

No one else but Cecil would do a thing like that, Mrs. Vista thought with nostalgia. She flipped over again on her side. Paula made a funny little noise which sounded like a sob.

"Why, you aren't sleeping!" Mrs. Vista said with great reproach.

"I am so!" Paula whispered savagely. "Leave me alone."

Mrs. Vista usually acted inversely to the wishes of other people. She raised herself on one elbow and squinted over at Paula. The tears were rolling down Paula's cheeks.

"Well, really!" said Mrs. Vista. "What are you crying about?"

"N-nothing."

"Nerves?" Mrs. Vista diagnosed. "I'm a great sufferer from nerves myself."

"It's not nerves," Paula said into her pillow. "I just want to go home."

Mrs. Vista sighed. "So do we all. A few more hours yet and we'll be on our way."

"I don't want to go to the lodge. I want to go *home*."

"What did you come for, in the first place?"

Paula rolled her head back and forth and sobbed into the pillow.

Mrs. Vista sighed and thought, she looked so quiet and thin. What a mistake! I should have taken a room to myself but this house seemed so eerie.

"I think you should go down to the bathroom and wash your face and stop this nonsense," she said firmly. "There's nothing like a dash of cold water . . ."

"Oh, be quiet," Paula said angrily and sat up and wiped off her tears with a handkerchief. "If I'm disturbing you, I'll go some place else. I'll go downstairs."

"You can't. Mr. Goodwin is sleeping down there."

Paula rolled off the bed. Like the others, she had not undressed and she looked very funny standing there dressed for skiing, her hair tousled and her eyes red from crying. Mrs. Vista began to laugh, holding her sides and rocking back and forth on the bed. Her laughter was punctuated by the banging of the radiator and the snores of Crawford coming from the next room.

Paula sat down again on the bed and tapped the floor with her foot. Mrs. Vista stopped laughing and said, "What time is it?"

"Midnight," Paula said shortly.

"What were you making all that fuss about?"

"Nothing. Homesick, I guess."

"Well, you didn't come here alone. Your cross young man . . ."

"He's not *my* young man. I've just known him since we were children. We're just *friends*."

Her eyes flickered, and even Mrs. Vista, who was no observer of human nature not her own, decided she was lying.

Paula rose and yawned. "I think I'll have that dash of cold water now. I have to take the lamp with me."

"Don't be long," Mrs. Vista said. "And close the door behind you."

Paula went out with the lamp. She was too engrossed in her own troubles to be nervous about the dark or to remember the dead cat.

She opened the bathroom door and went in. A trickle of pinkish brown water escaped from the tap. She dashed some on her face and dried it off with her last clean handkerchief.

She had her hand on the knob to go out again when she heard a faint scream. It seemed to come from nowhere. It was just there, like the howling of the wind, and then it was gone again.

Though it lasted only a second and was barely audible above the other noises, the scream was full of terror. It seemed to be torn from a throat that wouldn't scream again.

Her legs shaking, Paula walked quickly out into the hall. The doors were all shut, the house undisturbed and dark. No one else heard it, Paula thought. Perhaps I imagined it, or it was an animal outside . . .?

But she knew she had not imagined it when she went back to her room and found Mrs. Vista standing at the window, her face pale with fright.

"Did you hear it?" Mrs. Vista whispered huskily. "Did you hear someone scream?"

Paula nodded wordlessly.

"Someone died," Mrs. Vista said, putting her hand over her shaking mouth. "I feel it. I feel that someone is dead."

Chapter 6

"I FEEL IT," MRS. VISTA SAID AGAIN, WHILE CRAW-
ford's snoring rose to a crescendo and died into an echo.
"We'd better wake him up. Rap on his door."

"You come with me," Paula said.

For a full minute neither of them moved. Then Paula
took a long breath. "Are you coming? Someone's life may
be in danger."

She walked out and Mrs. Vista, trembling inside her huge
coat, followed her.

Paula rapped on Crawford's door. Almost instantly the
snoring ceased and a sharp alert voice called out, "Who's
there?"

"Open the door," Paula said.

When Crawford came to the door he was wearing his
overcoat and one hand rested in his pocket. His hair was
tangled from sleeping but his eyes were wide awake and
bright.

"What's up?" he said.

"We heard a scream," Paula said. "Someone screamed
and we don't know what to do about it. We thought—we
thought perhaps you could . . ." She stopped because Crawford was looking at her with such a dry, unconvinced smile.

"Yeah?" he said.

"We both heard it separately," Mrs. Vista said shrilly. "If
you don't intend to do something I'll wake the others."

She opened her mouth and began to shriek. "Help! Help!
Murder!"

Crawford was too late in putting his hand across her
mouth. He cursed at her softly when the doors started to
open along the hall.

Mrs. Vista took a deep breath, put her hands on Crawford's chest, and pushed. Crawford landed ungracefully on
one hip. There was a sharp clink of metal as he hit the
floor.

He picked himself up, wincing. He said, "You bitch," so
Mrs. Vista began to shriek again and the hall came alive

with lamps and people and resounded with the screams of Maudie and Mrs. Vista, and the roar of Miss Rudd pounding on the locked door.

Mr. Goodwin came leaping up the stairs like an overgrown gazelle, for he had recognized Mrs. Vista's voice, and poet or no poet he knew a good thing when he saw it and fifty thousand dollars a year must not perish. When he saw that Mrs. Vista was not perishing he decided to go back downstairs. But it was too late. Mrs. Vista had spied him and was flinging herself at him. Since Mrs. Vista weighed nearly two hundred pounds, Mr. Goodwin wisely propped himself against the brass banister railing and closed his eyes.

The impact came. Mr. Goodwin fancied he heard the crunch of bone. "There goes a vertebra," he muttered, and patted Mrs. Vista's shoulder.

The tumult gradually died down except for Miss Rudd's pounding, and Paula was able to explain what she had heard.

"But we're all here," Isobel said in a puzzled voice. "Nothing happened to any of us. We're all here."

"Except," Mr. Hunter said, "Floraine."

There was an uncomfortable silence. Then Isobel said, "Nothing could happen to Floraine. I mean, she's probably in Miss Rudd's room."

"That's easy to find out," Gracie said. "Just go in and look."

"She's locked in."

"We could smash in the door," said Herbert, who liked the idea since it was always being done in the stories he read.

"The doors are oak," Mr. Hunter said.

"Well, pick the lock," Gracie said with a shrug. "Or yell. Yell Floraine. Like this. FLORAINE!"

Miss Rudd also began to yell "Floraine!" evidently with a great deal of enjoyment.

After a couple of minutes of this Crawford went to the door and snarled, "Shut up in there!" Then he took out a pocket knife and pried at the lock.

The door swung open and revealed Miss Rudd in her gray flannel nightgown holding a chair over her head.

"Put that down," Crawford said.

Miss Rudd said nothing, but glared at him balefully.

"Put it down. I won't hurt you. I want to find Floraine."

The chair started to descend. Crawford stepped back and the chair crashed at his feet. He thrust the door shut and held his hands against it.

"She's strong as hell," he said through clenched teeth. "Somebody help me. Hunter. Put your back against it while I slip the lock back."

Mr. Hunter did as he was told. Crawford said, "The rest of you, get the hell back in your rooms."

The hall began to empty. Only Isobel remained, as if her feet were too heavy to move. She heard the lock slip back in place and felt herself trembling with relief.

Crawford turned from the door and saw her. "What are you doing here?"

"Admiring your versatility," Isobel said evenly. "And waiting to see Floraine."

Crawford smiled slightly. "I'd like to see her myself. I don't get along well with Miss Rudd."

Mr. Hunter said, "It's very queer she didn't hear this racket if she's around. You don't think she's had an accident?"

"I intend to find out," Isobel said.

"Because a couple of women imagined a scream?" Crawford said. "Go ahead and find out then. Search the house."

"If we'd had any men around with any courage we'd have searched it some time ago," Isobel said. "And if it's of any interest to you, Mr. Crawford, I already have done a little searching."

"With *my* flashlight?" Crawford said dryly. "Watch those light fingers, Isobel."

Flushing, Isobel continued. "And the driver *did* come here. I found parts of his clothing. And if you want to hear the rest of it, I think he's dead, do you understand? I think they *killed* him and you stand there raising your silly eyebrows and . . ." She broke off in a sob.

"Dear, dear," said Mr. Hunter. "Tut, tut. Don't cry."

"She's putting it all on," Crawford said in a hard voice. "I don't know what her game is . . ."

"Crawford, you're a brute," said Mr. Hunter.

"He's scared," Isobel said huskily. "He's scared silly."

"Oh, for God's sake," Crawford said. "All right. You want to search, all right let's search. What in hell you expect to find I don't know. Where's my flashlight?"

"I lent it to someone," Isobel confessed weakly.

"You are beginning," Crawford said gently, "to annoy me intensely."

He walked towards the staircase. Mr. Hunter hung back and looked wistful.

"Why don't you come too?" Isobel said. "Heaven knows we can't have too many." She raised her voice. "And I can't spend the whole night trying to persuade Mr. Crawford to put one foot in front of the other."

"Nuts," Crawford said. "Make it snappy. I'm tired."

"Tired?" Isobel said. "You're moribund."

"Mightn't it be a good idea to examine the third floor first?" Mr. Hunter suggested. "Make sure it's really shut up, I mean, a sort of process of elimination."

Isobel said, "Mr. Crawford, if you're not too tired, think that over, will you?"

"Sure," Crawford said. He turned around and led the way to the back staircase. It was enclosed, and the door was shut and padlocked. Mr. Hunter held his lamp directly over the padlock.

"Rusted," Isobel said. "Hasn't been used for years." She bent down and examined the sides of the door. The cracks had been filled in with putty.

"Nobody could get through here without a battering ram," Crawford said. "Now what? More eliminations? What, no suggestion from the little lady?"

"You talk too much," Isobel said coldly. "Obviously the next step is to go through all the bedrooms. She may be simply hiding. Had that occurred to you?"

"Last year," Crawford said. "How do you go about searching bedrooms?"

"Let's try yours first, shall we?"

"Sure," Crawford said. "Welcome, I'm sure."

Crawford's bedroom was small and without a clothes closet or fireplace. There was obviously no place anyone could hide except under the bed. And there Isobel looked, her face reddening under Crawford's exaggerated leer. He said, "T-t-t-t. Sorry, Isobel. Better luck next time."

Nothing of interest came to light in the bedrooms except Maudie Thropple's beautiful bridgework which had been removed to prevent her swallowing it while in a faint.

There remained Miss Rudd's bedroom but no one seemed eager to tackle it, least of all Crawford who said it would upset all his favorite ideas of how he was going to commit suicide some day. So they went downstairs.

Mr. Goodwin was giving his insomnia a workout in front of the fire.

He said, "Well?" rather aggressively.

"We want to search this room," Isobel explained. "Mr. Crawford, could you take that side and I'll take this side with Mr. Hunter."

"What about me?" Mr. Goodwin said.

"All we ask from you is a cosy silence," Crawford re-

plied. He began to creep around the room, patting the chesterfield cushions and peering behind the drapes saying, "Ah!"

Isobel gritted her teeth and tried hard not to pay any
attention, but Crawford's "Ah's!" became too loud to ignore.

"Stop your clowning," she said sternly.

"Hell, I was just getting into the spirit of the thing,"
Crawford said.

"If you think this is a joke you'd better not come with
us."

"I do think it's a joke. If I ever saw a woman better able
to take care of herself than Floraine . . ." He stopped and
shrugged. "Oh, come on. You lady detectives kill me."

He went out first. Mr. Hunter, after whispering something soothing but inaudible in Isobel's ear, followed him.

The room across the hall turned out to be a library. It
hadn't been used for years, evidently, as the furniture was
covered with dust sheets and the sheets themselves were
grimy. Only one shelf of books remained. Isobel picked one
out and opened it, closing it hastily when a couple of book-
worms stirred themselves and started to move across the
page. The binding of the book was mildewed. Isobel replaced
it on the shelf and looked at the titles of the rest of them.
Historical books, mostly, with one or two on local geography
and a vast tome on how to recognize and cure your own
ailments. Isobel would have liked to sit down and pick herself out a couple of ailments and worry over them; but
business before pleasure, she told herself firmly, and began
swatting at the dust sheets in the faint hope that Floraine
would be underneath one of them.

But Floraine was not in the library. Nor, it developed,
was she in the dining room. In the hall closet Mr. Hunter
turned up a pair of old snowshoes and in the kitchen Crawford found a bottle of brandy, but Floraine remained elusive.

Crawford wanted to open the brandy on the theory that
it would provide inspiration for all. Isobel objected. Mr.
Hunter wavered, then catching Isobel's cold eye, he also
objected. Crawford put the bottle in his pocket.

"Are you sure you have room for it?" Isobel said sweetly.
"Sure it won't load you down when you're carrying your
arsenal?"

"I'll put it in the *other* pocket," Crawford said.

Mr. Hunter looked from one to the other. "I don't quite
follow . . ."

"That's all right," Crawford said. "Nobody can keep any
secrets from our Isobel."

Mr. Hunter was beginning to show signs of strain. He kept pulling violently at his mustache.

"I wish she'd turn up some place," he said. "I mean to say, there's only one more floor, and if she's not in the house, where is she?"

They looked, simultaneously, out of the kitchen window. There was nothing to be seen but the snow beating on the window.

Isobel swallowed hard and said, "She wouldn't have gone out. She'd die in this blizzard. She must be here some place."

"Miss Lashley said the scream was very faint," Mr. Hunter said. "That might mean it came from the cellar."

"Well, let's go," Crawford said, and opened the door into the cellar.

In the main room Isobel's eye fell on the two trunks that Joyce had said were empty. She opened the lids of both and found that Joyce, as usual, had been right. She examined the floor—solid concrete, impossible to bury a body here—and then followed Crawford into the furnace room.

She saw that Crawford was staring intently at the furnace and that he was no longer amused.

"She put the cat in there," Isobel said weakly. "You don't suppose . . ."

"Take a look at the size of the door," Crawford said roughly. "You couldn't get a body in there unless you cut it up into steaks."

Mr. Hunter looked green and said, "Really. I must ask you . . ." His voice faded.

"Try cutting up somebody and you get blood," Crawford said. "And there's no blood."

"Please," Mr. Hunter bleated.

"There's only one other place," Isobel said. "Under the coal."

Crawford eyed her grimly. "Yeah? And that means?"

"I'm afraid it means," Isobel said in a small voice, "that you shovel."

Crawford flung his arms around. "Oh, hell. This is too much. This is what I get for treating you civilly. . . ."

Mr. Hunter unexpectedly took his side. "I do think it's a bit drastic. Must be six or seven tons of coal here. Devilish job. And what—what if we *find* something?"

Isobel's mouth tightened. "This is exactly what I expected from both of you. You are a pair of incompetent, ineffectual, muddling little sissies."

"Oh, come, come," said Mr. Hunter feebly.

"I should bat you around," Crawford said, "but I'm too damn tired. Good night, all."

He moved to the door.

"You mean to say," Isobel spluttered, "you mean to say you're actually going to bed? You'd leave *me* to shovel six or seven tons of coal, you cad?"

"Let them as wants to shovel, shovel," Crawford said. "I'm C.I.O. and can't work after midnight."

"All right, I will!" Isobel shouted.

Crawford's voice floated back from the other room. "Scab."

They heard him go up the steps, whistling. Speechless with rage, Isobel swung round and faced Mr. Hunter. Mr. Hunter, recognizing the symptoms, started to back away from her with a sickly smile on his face.

"This," Isobel said at last, using the illogical reasoning powers of her sex, "is all your fault."

"Oh now, come. I didn't do a . . ."

"Hand me that shovel."

"No, I couldn't, really . . ."

"Hand me that shovel!"

Mr. Hunter wisely handed her the shovel and backed away again.

"And now, if you don't mind," Isobel said, "you may go upstairs. I have no intention of shoveling coal in front of a witness."

"I couldn't leave you here," Mr. Hunter protested. "If there's any kind of danger I'd like to share it with you. And I can shovel a bit too, I suppose."

It was not a tactful speech. Isobel shouted, "Go away!" and hurled herself at the coal pile.

Mr. Hunter went away and crept guiltily back upstairs.

Ten minutes later Isobel removed her coat and fifteen minutes after that she took off the jacket of her suit. Her nose and throat smarted from the coal dust, and when she put her hand up to wipe the sweat from her forehead it left two long black streaks. But she kept on shoveling, driven by her anger, and eventually she had the satisfaction of seeing that the small pile was growing even if the large pile didn't appear to be decreasing.

She rested on the shovel a moment. When she straightened up pains shot through her back and her hands were starting to blister, and, what was worse, she was beginning to flag mentally. The whole thing was preposterous, even if two people *had* disappeared. There might be a secret door or something—something . . .

She straightened up once more. A little avalanche of coal

slid from the big pile and touched her feet. When the cellar was quiet again a voice spoke directly behind her:

"How are you doing?"

She gasped and dropped the shovel and turned around to meet Crawford's eyes.

"Tsk, tsk," Crawford said. "Still mad."

"Not mad," Isobel said coldly. "Disgusted."

"Here. Give me the shovel. You've had your workout."

"No, thank you. I'll do it myself. You're far too delicate for this kind of work."

"Don't be proud," Crawford said. "Your face is dirty."

"Well, it's good, honest dirt!" Isobel shouted.

"Dirt," said Crawford, "is dirt," and he gave her a hand-kerchief and took the shovel out of her hands.

He started shoveling very blithely. Isobel sat on the work bench and watched gloatingly for the first signs of tiredness. Now and then she called out encouragement: "Oooh! That was a big one! My, aren't you strong?"

After a time he stood up and said, "Isobel. You still think this is a good idea?"

"I do."

"All right. I just wanted to know."

Half an hour later he said, "Isobel, you're a woman of iron determination. How about let's compromise? We'll go to bed now and finish up in the morning."

"Put some coal on the fire while you're at it," Isobel said calmly. "It's getting chilly in here. Or don't you think so?"

Crawford, already down to his shirt, said no, he didn't think so.

It was two o'clock when he laid down the shovel. The two piles were even now. The rest, Crawford said, could be prodded with a poker.

Some time later they went upstairs together. Neither of them said anything. Isobel was pale and close to tears. Over Crawford's one arm hung a coat of heavy tan wool with a strip of cloth sewn to the under side of the collar. On the cloth was printed in India ink: "Maurice Hearst. Chateau Neige, Quebec."

There was no sign of Floraine.

Chapter 7

THEY PAUSED IN FRONT OF THE SITTING-ROOM door. Crawford kept brushing at the coat absently, and raising little clouds of dust.

"What are you going to do?" Isobel said.

"Wash."

"About the coat."

He looked across at her. "What can I do? Put it in a closet, I guess, and forget it."

"You can't forget it," Isobel said hoarsely. "You've got some responsibility."

"Not a scrap. Me for me is my motto."

"And you won't take charge of anything?"

"There's nothing to take charge of, so far."

"Isn't there?" Isobel said. "A bunch of strangers marooned in a house with a crazy woman and the nurse gone?"

"We'll be out of here as soon as it's light," Crawford said.

"Leaving Miss Rudd alone?"

"What do you expect me to do, give her a piggy-back ride?"

"You know we can't leave her alone here. It would be inhuman."

"All right, so I'm inhuman—and tired—and dirty . . . Good night."

He strode impatiently down the hall and opened the door of the closet where Mr. Hunter had found the snowshoes. He threw the coat inside and closed the door again and made for the stairs. When he was halfway to the top Isobel called softly, "Charles!"

He took two more steps and turned around, frowning.

Isobel said, "You're not very used to your name. How long have you had it?"

"About twelve hours," Crawford said easily.

"You look older than that," Isobel said.

"I am, but don't tell anybody. Good night."

Isobel went slowly into the sitting room. Mr. Goodwin had gone to sleep again, so she sat in front of the fire and thought, there's only one other place Floraine could be. She could be in Miss Rudd's room. Probably the rifle that she used is in there too, since we didn't find it.

Miss Rudd and a rifle and Floraine, dead or alive, behind one locked door . . .

But there had been no shot, only the one faint scream. Isobel thought of the balcony along the second floor and wondered if there could be some way of looking into Miss Rudd's room without unlocking the door. But the balcony was probably unsafe, and she couldn't go out anyway in this blizzard.

She frowned into the fire and thought, in spite of the cat and the chair flung at Crawford I'm not really *afraid* of Miss Rudd.

She examined this thought and promptly dismissed it as a lie. I'm afraid of her, she decided, but I can't accept her actions as purely evil. She doesn't realize what she's doing. She can be managed, as Floraine managed her. If I could get sort of unemotionally tough . . .

She put more wood on the fire, poked it once or twice, and went to the door. When she passed Crawford's door she heard him snoring already, sleeping the sleep of the just, the pure and the clear of conscience. Highly incensed, she passed on into her own room.

Gracie was sitting up on the bed, looking cheerful.

"Look!" she said brightly.

So Isobel looked and saw Miss Rudd squatting on the floor beside the bed. Miss Rudd, too, looked cheerful. She was chewing the rest of Gracie's chocolates.

"The poor old thing said she was hungry," Gracie said. "Reminds me of the aunt I told you about, always hungry she was." She turned to Miss Rudd. "Now take it easy. One at a time like I told you."

Isobel said in a faraway voice: "Gracie. How did she . . .? I mean, how . . .?"

"Oh. That. Well, there she was, the poor dear, pounding and pounding on that door, just like that aunt of mine again. So I let her out. We get along fine, don't we, Frances?"

Frances nodded pleasantly.

"Was—was Floraine in there with her?" Isobel said.

"No," Gracie said. "Just the rifle. She was playing with it, so I took it away from her and threw it out the window. Was that the right thing to do?"

"Oh, yes," Isobel said, gulping. "Oh, yes, yes."

"Come on. Sit down. Just like a party practically, isn't it?"

"Just," Isobel said, and sat down because she was too

weak to stand. Gracie lit a cigarette and let Miss Rudd blow out the match.

There was a silence, friendly on the part of Miss Rudd and Gracie, stupefied on the part of Isobel. She decided that Gracie, in her way, was strongly akin to Miss Rudd, hence the bond between them.

"I told her Floraine was gone," Gracie said. "She just laughed. I don't think Floraine was good to her."

Miss Rudd shook her head violently and made a few unprintable remarks on Floraine's character.

"See?" Gracie said. "She's quite sensible."

"Just like your aunt," Isobel said. "The three of you ought to get together sometime."

"What do you think we should do now?" Gracie said. "It's nearly three. It should be light in five hours. I suppose we could all just sit here and talk."

"I'm afraid I'd be conscious of some strain," Isobel said.

Miss Rudd had finished the chocolates. She wiped her mouth on her shawl and came over to the bed. She touched Gracie's hair with her finger.

"Like it?" Gracie said, without a tremor. "It used to be brown, but brown doesn't suit me, I'm too vivid. Go on, sit down again, Frances."

Miss Rudd smiled, almost shyly. "I have something for you," she whispered in Gracie's ear. She rolled her eyes.

"That's swell," Gracie said. "What is it?"

"Something," said Miss Rudd.

"Is it a secret?"

Miss Rudd nodded vigorously. "I took it from Floraine. I took it from her desk."

"Where is it?"

For answer Miss Rudd darted to the door and out into the hall.

Isobel said, "Come back. Frances! Please come back."

"Let her alone," Gracie said easily. "She'll come back. She can even see in the dark like my . . ."

"Please," Isobel said.

"I hope it's a bottle of rye."

But it was not a bottle of rye. It was a bunch of old newspapers, some of them badly torn.

"Gee, thanks," Gracie said, taking the newspapers. "Just what I wanted. Something to read. Here, Isobel, have one. You want to read too, Frances?"

Miss Rudd did. She sat down again on the floor holding one of the papers stiffly in front of her.

Gracie looked curiously at the rest of the papers. "Wonder why Floraine would save these."

"She's the type who'd save anything. Give me that one." Isobel reached for it.

That one turned out to be the *Montreal Star*. It was dated September 3, 1942.

"Quite a little reader, our Floraine," Isobel said, *"Montreal Star. Ottawa Citizen. Quebec Courier* . . . Gracie, what's the date on yours?"

"September 4, 1942."

"Look through the others."

There were twelve papers altogether. Each one bore the date September 3rd or September 4th. Five of them were in French and looked like small-town newspapers and came from places Isobel had never heard of.

"That's funny," she said. "Move the lamp closer and we'll look through them all. Something must have happened on September the third that interested Floraine very much. She's not the type who saves paper for the war effort."

"How about 'R.A.F. Raid Over Germany' or 'Wife Clubbed to Death by Hired Man'? And here's the picture of kind of a cute man. I'm crazy about little dark mustaches, only he probably hasn't got his now, he's in jail."

Isobel leaned over and looked at Gracie's cute man. Miss Rudd put down her paper and came over too. Her mouth moved as if she were reading silently to herself. But Isobel knew she was not reading, her eyes didn't move but remained fixed on the picture.

"Go on, Frances," Gracie said. "Stop pushing. Do you want this one? Go on, take it then." Gracie thrust the paper at her and picked up another one, yawning. "I still wish I had a bottle of rye. I never did like reading."

"Here's your cute man again," Isobel said. "Demoted to page five this time. He looks familiar, doesn't he?"

"Like Cary Grant," Gracie said dreamily. "What's his name?"

"Pierre Jeanneret."

"I think that's sweet. I wonder why he's in jail."

"He talked too much," Isobel said. She quoted from the news item: " 'Jeanneret, long known as a political agitator, was apprehended at Montreal while leading a student riot against conscription. He was interned for the duration under the Defense of Canada Regulations. As he was led from the court . . .' "

"More chocolates," said Miss Rudd, who was easily bored.

"Haven't any," Gracie said.

"I'm hungry. I'm a poor, hungry, old lady, and I want some more chocolates."

"Hush. We'll be having breakfast in a few hours."

"Harry stole all my food," Miss Rudd whined. "He comes in the night and Floraine locks me up."

"Now don't get excited," Gracie said pleasantly. "Floraine's not going to lock you up tonight."

Miss Rudd giggled suddenly. Isobel didn't like the sound of it.

"You don't know what happened to Floraine?" she said, keeping her voice calm.

"She's gone," said Miss Rudd, "and she won't be back." She came over to the bed and began to stroke Isobel's coat. "Pretty. Very soft and pretty, like Etienne."

Isobel sat rigid.

"You give me this coat," Miss Rudd whispered. "You give it to me, eh?"

"No, no, I can't. I'd be cold without it."

"I'm cold. Harry's friends took all my coal. I heard them. I'll be very cold without this coat."

Gracie said, "Look, Frances. I have a pretty necklace for you. You want it?"

Miss Rudd's hands darted out for the necklace. Then, whispering to herself, she slipped out into the hall again. She was gone a long time.

Isobel said nervously, "I wonder what she's doing."

"Hiding it," Gracie said. "My aunt used to hide everything like that."

"I'm getting a little tired of your aunt."

"Well, we did too," Gracie said, "but she finally died."

"I think we should go out and look for Frances. You shouldn't have let her out of her room. She may be all right when she's with you, but the rest of us haven't had your experience."

"Oh, she'll come back. Anyway, I can't go skipping around with fur mittens on my feet. Just leave her alone."

"We left her alone before," Isobel said, "and something happened to Etienne. I can't understand you. You're scared to death to search the house and yet you let Miss Rudd out of her room. You have no sense of proportion."

"Maybe not," Gracie said.

"Unless you did it deliberately."

"What?"

"Let Miss Rudd out."

"Sure, I did it deliberately. It's not the kind of thing

you do in your sleep. I felt sorry for her. She was hungry and . . ."

"I don't believe it," Isobel said.

Gracie turned her head. Her eyes were narrowed and she was smiling. "You don't believe what? And who cares?"

"You let her out to start trouble."

"Now who's starting trouble?" Gracie shrugged her shoulders. "God knows *I* don't want any."

Isobel stared at her a minute, then dropped her eyes.

Perhaps she really is that dumb, she thought, perhaps she didn't realize what she was doing and actually felt sorry for Miss Rudd.

No, I don't believe it. She couldn't have forgotten the dead cat, she was terrified at the blood on her stockings.

Gracie's voice broke abruptly into her thoughts:

"Since we're going to be suspicious of each other, would you mind telling me what a dame like you is doing up here?"

"I want to learn to ski," Isobel said.

"So you had to come all the way up here?"

Isobel blushed and said, "I read an advertisement. They teach by a special method and the ad said you could learn in a week and they have an ex-Austrian ski-meister . . ."

"His name is Schultz," Gracie said, "and he comes from a village in Ontario and the nearest he's been to Austria is the World's Fair."

"I don't believe it!"

"He got me this job," Gracie said. "You'd better stop reading ads. You're the type who cries for Castoria when you're a baby, switches to Ex-Lax at seven, chews Feena-mint until you're twenty-one, and spends the rest of your life eating All-Bran."

Miss Rudd chose this tense moment to reappear in the doorway. She had been on quite a tour evidently, for she had picked up several stale buns, half a loaf of bread and a man's tie. The tie Isobel recognized as Mr. Goodwin's.

"A strange house," said Mr. Goodwin, fingering the place where his tie had once been knotted. "A very, very, very strange house."

Mr. Goodwin was a far from ordinary man and had found himself in some far from ordinary places in his thirty-two years, but until today no one had ever shot at him or cut his hat into ribbons or stolen a tie from his sleeping and defenseless neck. Nor, until tonight, had Mr. Goodwin ever been released from the torments of insomnia, nor so deserted by his muse.

The cat, for instance, was well worth a quatrain of blood-imagery, but try as he would Mr. Goodwin could get no further than the title, simple but telling, "Cat."

He sat up straight on the chesterfield and peered into the darkness for signs of the creeping fingers he had felt around his throat. He saw nothing, which was fortunate, for he was not cast in the heroic mold, and preferred to be a mystic rather than take the trouble to find out facts. Faced with the choice of believing in Miss Rudd or pixies, Mr. Goodwin chose pixies and was the happier for it.

There was, however, the sound of someone walking in the hall and the footfall was rather heavier than you would expect even from the best-nourished pixie.

Still, why seek the disaster of enlightenment? Mr. Goodwin lay down again and closed his eyes. The footsteps were not stealthy, they had a determined briskness about them, which to Mr. Goodwin's mind meant either Evaline Vista or Isobel Seton. He did not feel able to cope with either of these ladies at present, so he closed his eyes more tightly. This proved to be his undoing.

"You're not sleeping," said a cool voice right above his head. "Your eyes are all squinty. You can't fool me."

"Obviously not," said Mr. Goodwin wearily and sat up again.

Joyce Hunter, very bright-eyed and trim in the brown slack suit she'd worn under her skiing clothes, sat down beside him.

"People," she said, "have been rushing up and down the hall upstairs. So I thought I'd better get up and see what's doing, but as soon as *I* got up the people were gone. Isn't that funny?"

"No," said Mr. Goodwin.

"One of them was Miss Seton. She's very spry for her age, I think. I hope she doesn't get any ideas about Poppa."

"Ideas?"

"Marriage. You know. Poppa's a frightful ass in some ways. I always have to rescue him. I wonder where Miss Rudd is. Somebody let her out."

"Why don't you go and look for her?" Mr. Goodwin said coaxingly. "Wouldn't that be fun?"

"No," Joyce said, "and please stop treating me as a child. I'm nineteen. People are fully adult at nineteen. Think back to yourself at nineteen."

Mr. Goodwin thought back to himself at nineteen and shuddered, with reason.

"Well, anyway," Joyce said, "I certainly didn't feel like

staying up in my room all alone with Miss Rudd running around loose. Perhaps I'll stay here for the rest of the night. We could talk about poetry, unless you'd rather tell me about your affairs."

"No," said Mr. Goodwin, "I wouldn't."

"I'd be terribly interested. A lot of people confide in me, I'm so close-mouthed. Not even one affair, just to pass the time?"

"Well, perhaps one," Mr. Goodwin said grudgingly. "Have you heard about Lady Hamilton-Fyske and myself?"

"No," Joyce breathed, blinking her eyes rapidly.

"Cecily was very impetuous," Mr. Goodwin mused. "She had everything, beauty, money, figure, honorable mention in *Who's Who* and an I.Q. of one-forty. Her husband was in the House of Lords, of course, a big sporting fellow who went in for hunting and drinking. Once when he was hunting in the Congo he shot off all his bearers just for the thrill of trying to get out of the Congo by himself."

Joyce frowned and said, "Really?"

"Really," Mr. Goodwin said firmly. "Naturally Cecily had a lot of time on her hands so she took up the study of Sanskrit. That was how I met her. She was in the British Museum sobbing bitterly over the defunct present participle of the verb, to be."

"You're making this up," Joyce said in stiff, dignified tones.

Mr. Goodwin sighed and stared up at the ceiling. "Best I could do."

"I bet you've never even *had* an affair."

"Let's talk about you," Mr. Goodwin said. "What are you going to be when you grow up?"

Joyce gazed at him sulkily.

"Because if you've nothing else in mind," Mr. Goodwin said gently, "I think there's a fine career ahead of you as a Public Enemy."

"Oh, you're just trying to make me mad," Joyce said with a sniff, "so I'll go off to bed. That won't work. Besides, I'm too hungry to sleep. I wish I had some food. I know where there is some."

At the mention of food Mr. Goodwin realized that he too was very hungry. A bargain was eventually struck whereby Joyce would procure food in return for being treated as a civilized and intelligent adult. Mr. Goodwin thought he was worsted in the bargain, but when Joyce returned with an opened can of beans and some bread he decided to let it ride. The beans were cold, but they gave Mr. Goodwin a warm glow in the pit of his muse. He produced an item called "Snow," which, while not first-rate, definitely showed the Goodwin flair.

> "Snow snow snow.
>   The white of it and the fright of it.
>   The delight of it and the blight of it.
>   The might of it.
>   Hélas, the neige is beige."

This was as far as he got. Still, it was definitely encouraging. The muse was not dead, she had merely a touch of hypochondria.

Cheered, Mr. Goodwin recited it to Joyce. Joyce said it stank.

"Really?" said Mr. Goodwin, pleased. "Really stinks?"

"Terribly."

Mr. Goodwin knew then that he had achieved success. He hastily wrote it down on the back of a bill for Dental Services, Dr. Gratton, fifteen dollars, please remit.

He was interrupted by the breathless arrival of Isobel Seton. Isobel was looking rather worn. When she saw Goodwin her face sagged with relief.

"Thank God," she said. "You're all right?"

Mr. Goodwin was fine and said so, feeling extremely pleased at Isobel's reaction to this announcement.

"I thought you were dead," she explained. "I mean Miss Rudd came in with your tie and I thought, we thought—maybe you were strangled."

"Strangled?" said Mr. Goodwin, shaken.

Isobel drew in her breath and began again. "I mean, Miss Rudd came to me with your tie and we didn't see . . . Oh, the hell with it!"

She flounced over to a chair and sank into it. "Here, take the thing," she said, flinging his tie to him. "And for heaven's sake hang on to your clothes."

"Who let her out?" Joyce said.

"Gracie Morning."

"Oh," Joyce said thoughtfully. "Why?"

"Humanitarian reasons," Isobel said grimly. "You figure it out."

"She's all right, is she? Not homicidal or anything?"

"Not yet."

"What's she doing?" Joyce asked.

"Reading. Reading some papers. She stole the papers from Floraine's desk and brought them as a present to Gracie.

And please don't ask me any more questions, Miss Hunter, because I can't answer them."

Joyce said huffily, "Well, if you can't, who can? You've been tearing up and down the hall upstairs all night."

"Mr. Crawford and I found the bus-driver's coat under the coal."

Joyce's eyes gleamed for an instant. "You did? What did Mr. Crawford do with it?"

"Put it in the closet in the hall."

"May I see it?"

"Why?" Isobel said.

"Can't I do some snooping as well as you?"

There was a lively argument on snooping powers which ended in Joyce's going out to look at the coat.

She came back looking cross. "It's not there," she announced. "Miss Rudd must have beat us to it."

Chapter 8

MAUDIE THROPPLE AWOKE WITH THE STRONG conviction that somebody was chasing somebody else through the hall. There was the scuffling of feet and several small squeals, followed by a thud and the sound of feet going violently down the steps. Under normal circumstances Maudie might have had hysterics at these odd noises, but she had lived through a great deal today. Her cup was full, and anything more that happened to her was bound to be an anticlimax.

So she merely raised herself from the pillow and nudged Herbert in the back with her elbow.

She said in the frail voice required of a woman who has fainted twice in one evening: "Herbie. Herbie dear, wake up."

Herbie dear tried his best not to wake up, but Maudie had a sharp insistent elbow which she used with unerring accuracy. Herbert groaned aloud.

Maudie felt that the groan was an insult to her status as an invalid. She abandoned the frail voice for something more compelling.

"You might at least wake up when I tell you to, after what I've been through, Herbert. There's someone fighting in the hall."

"You've been dreaming," Herbert said hopefully. When a cold silence greeted this remark he sat up on the bed and listened. The hall was quiet. He said, "You're just excited. Lie down again, angel. Take it easy."

Maudie could think of no reply scathing enough. She looked across at the man with whom she had chosen to spend the rest of her years. Chosen. No compulsion about it.

Herbert did not measure up. Perhaps in a cosy restaurant, wearing a dinner coat and nicely shaved and combed with a little talcum to tone down the highlights in his bald spot —*perhaps* . . .

But seen in the light of an oil lamp, swaddled in moth-eaten blankets, Herbert failed to meet the test. His hair seemed to sprout above his ears, not like hair at all but like a strange fungus growth. His eyes were half-closed and there was none of that steely glint in them that proclaimed: Here is a man.

I have made, Maudie thought, Another Mistake. She shuddered.

"Cold, angel?" said Herbert.

"Get up," Maudie said. "Go and look in the hall. And don't call me silly names."

Herbert knew this mood well. He hastily disentangled himself from the blankets and went to the door. The hall was very dark and he might have missed Miss Rudd entirely if she had not opened the conversation by saying, "I pinched Harry."

"You did, eh?" Herbert said nervously. "Well, well."

Behind him Maudie's voice said anxiously, "Who is it?"

"Oh, it's nothing," Herbert said. "Nothing much."

Miss Rudd was sitting on the floor in the hall. She had had a big night and was looking tired but happy.

"I pinched Harry," she said, "and he pushed me and ran away down the steps. *What* a coward!"

"Shut that door," Maudie hissed. "Shut it! It's her again!"

Herbert said, "Well, good night," and shut the door.

"She's loose," Maudie said. "Someone let her loose."

"She seems to be all right, though," said Herbert, who could spot a silver lining miles away. "She's not into anything. Might as well let her alone."

"You'll have to do something!"

"What can I do? She wouldn't listen to me anyway."

"We can't just stay here."

The problem was solved by the rather breathless arrival of Paula Lashley.

She said, "Mr. Crawford thinks we should all get up and go downstairs and stay together. It's six o'clock anyway, and most of the others are down there."

"They left us alone up here," cried Maudie with a tragic gesture.

"Nonsense," Paula said coolly. "Chad and Mr. Hunter are right across the hall."

She went out again, passing Miss Rudd who gazed at her brightly but said nothing.

She rapped on Chad's door. She could hear someone getting off the bed and soon Chad came and opened the door. He had just wakened up and his eyes were soft and the scowl hadn't appeared on his face yet.

She said softly, "Hello."

He smiled at her gently, and for a minute everything was all right. Then Miss Rudd stirred, and Paula lowered her eyes.

"The others are downstairs. Mr. Crawford thinks we should go down too."

"Paula . . ."

"Don't say anything. I don't want to talk about anything."

"You never do!" He gripped her shoulders tightly. "You're an awful coward."

"Take your hands off me."

He released her shoulders.

"You can't solve everything by force," Paula said levelly. "You'd better wake Mr. Hunter. I'm going down."

"I could solve it by force if I wanted to, but I'm beginning to think you're not worth the trouble. You want to go back, all right go back. Only don't write me any sniveling little notes asking me . . ."

"You won't get any notes." She turned and walked stiffly down the stairs.

Chad went back into his room and found Mr. Hunter sitting up with every appearance of having enjoyed the snatch of conversation.

"Women," he said sadly, "are difficult to understand, my boy. Even a man of my years occasionally finds himself at a loss."

This was a plain case of understatement, but Mr. Hunter was unaware of it and Chad didn't care to point it out. He growled something in return and started to smooth down his hair.

"If there's anything I can help you with," Mr. Hunter

said, "anything requiring experience in these matters such as I . . ."

"Thanks, no."

"Just ask my advice if anything turns up," Mr. Hunter said wistfully. "I can't say that I'm much help to my own family. Joyce seems to be a very competent girl."

"We're supposed to be going downstairs," Chad said. "What for, I don't know. I was doing all right up here."

Mr. Hunter looked mournful. "Probably Miss Seton is at the bottom of it. She's one of these women who gets ideas and then expects other people to carry them out. The very worst type, take my word for it."

"I will," Chad said abruptly. "Coming?"

"I suppose I'll have to."

In the sitting room Mr. Hunter's fears were realized. Isobel had taken a stance in front of the fireplace and she was looking both angry and determined. She said in the brisk voice of a woman accustomed to giving commands to horses, dogs and men:

"Are we all here?"

"Miss Morning isn't," said Mrs. Vista.

"She's upstairs with Miss Rudd," Isobel said. "Mr. Crawford and I decided . . ."

"You decided," Crawford said.

". . . that we had better meet to decide what we're going to do about Floraine and how we're going to get out of here this morning as soon as it's light."

"I don't think we should worry about getting out of here," Herbert said. "The people at the lodge will have sent out a party looking for the bus and when they find the bus they'll trace us here."

"You have more confidence in people who run lodges than I have," said Isobel coldly, "and much more confidence in the bus-driver. How do we know that he was even taking us to the lodge? How do we know he was on the right road? It seemed to me that the road was nothing more than a lane. Has anyone been to this place before?"

"I have," Paula said. "I was here last year, but I can't remember the road that well."

"I think," Isobel continued, "that he turned off the right road, that it was all part of a plan to get us here in this house."

"To get us here?" Herbert echoed. "But that's fantastic! I mean, why should anyone want us here? Why, we don't even know each other."

"No, we don't," Isobel said slowly. "None of us know anything about each other."

"I wish you wouldn't talk like that," Mrs. Vista said loudly. "Here we are and we have to stand each other anyway, so I don't think we should inquire too closely. My life is an open book, of course, but I don't care to have it a best-seller."

"I can see I'm going to get very little cooperation," Isobel said.

"You're going to get none, sister," said Crawford.

Isobel raised her eyebrows. "Mr. Crawford is an interesting case to start with. In the first place his name is not Crawford. In the second, he's carrying a gun. In the third, he deliberately destroyed a piece of evidence that the bus-driver actually came to this house."

"You forgot the bottle of brandy," Crawford said cheerfully. "I stole it from the kitchen."

Isobel flushed. "You admit the other things?"

"I admit everything."

"How Oxford-Groupish," said Mrs. Vista. "These things get very embarrassing sometimes. I remember in London once . . ."

"That's a fact about the brandy, is it?" Herbert said with interest. "I don't suppose you'd care to pass it around?"

"Not sanitary," said Crawford.

"Please!" Isobel shouted. "If you're all going to launch into private conversations how are we going to decide anything? I gave Mr. Crawford as an example. He may have his reasons for this extraordinary behavior, and as far as I know it's no crime to change your name. But the point is *he* could easily be the one who arranged this set-up, for all we know about him."

"But he was the one who tried to start the bus again," Maudie said.

"And failed," Isobel said dryly.

"Don't get into an argument over me, ladies," Crawford said, grinning. "I'm not worth it."

Chad Ross leaned forward in his chair. "Just why are you carrying a gun, Crawford?"

"I'm an international spy," Crawford said. "And I have a license."

"Yeah?" Chad said. "Let's see it."

"Come and get it," Crawford said in a hard voice, "if you want a clip, Redhead."

"I've been clipped before. It doesn't take."

"Please!" Isobel shouted again.

"Yes, yes," Mr. Hunter said. "A little more attention, please. These are grave matters."

"Oh, be quiet, Poppa," Joyce said petulantly. "I wanted to see if he really would clip him."

"That girl," said Mrs. Vista, "is a troublemaker if I ever saw one. I consider clipping very vulgar myself. If there's any to be done, kindly advise me and I shall leave the room. You too, Anthony."

The crisis passed and Isobel was able to continue. She seemed, however, to have lost the thread of her discourse and started in on personalities.

"The difficulty is," she said heatedly, "that you're all too bone-selfish to care what happens to anyone else. You don't care that two people have disappeared from this house. You don't care what happens to Miss Rudd. You'd all walk out and leave her here with no one to look after her!"

"Oh, I wouldn't!" said Mrs. Vista, shocked. "I'd leave Miss Morning here too."

"Please keep quiet. Personally, I don't want to sit around and wait to be rescued. Mr. Hunter has found a pair of snowshoes and I think one of us should go out and get help. It's a matter of a few miles . . ."

"A few miles in what direction?" Crawford said. "And don't look at me. If you think I'm going to do penance for my life of sin by rescuing a bunch of crackpots . . ."

"Who's a crackpot?" Chad said with menace.

"Oh, it's you again, is it? You still want that clip? Or do you want to go snowshoeing?"

Isobel shouted, "As for direction, that's easy enough. Go in the direction the bus was pointed towards."

"Even if he was on the wrong road," Crawford said. "That sounds fine. You have a very peculiar mind, Isobel. Your left brain lobe doesn't know what your right brain lobe is thinking up. Let's have no more of this tripe. Action, I don't mind. I'll tear up floorboards and crawl down drainpipes looking for Floraine, but no snowshoes."

"Well, why don't *you* suggest something?" Isobel cried.

"As much as I'd like to get away from the all-too-familiar pans which surround me, I can make only one concrete suggestion. Breakfast."

"We haven't settled anything yet!" Isobel said, but Crawford's suggestion was too near to the hearts of the others and Isobel found herself without supporters.

There was a general exodus to the kitchen. Mr. Hunter stayed behind to comfort Isobel.

"I think everything you said was perfectly right," he said, giving her shoulder a timid pat.

"Well, everything I said wasn't perfectly right," Isobel said crossly.

"All the more reason why you should be flattered," Mr. Hunter said with an enigmatic look, and followed the rest of them out the door. Isobel arrived in the kitchen in time to hear the news that the stove was an electric one and wouldn't work.

There was, however, a small battered-looking wood range which Herbert volunteered to light. The question of what to cook and who was to cook it turned out to be a delicate one. All of the ladies present claimed to be at a complete loss in a kitchen, with Joyce going them one better and insisting she had never even *seen* a kitchen before.

Mr. Hunter was considerably agitated and said, "Tut, tut. Surely we must have one *womanly* woman in the group."

He looked at Isobel, who returned the look well laced with vinegar.

"Anyone can make toast or something," he said anxiously.

"I can't," Isobel said firmly.

"I don't even know what toast is," said Joyce, who always won.

Mrs. Vista said that even in her country home in Sussex where life was at its most rigorous, she had never made toast. The scullery maid made it, passed it to the cook for approval or veto, then gave it to the second footman to convey to the table.

"The fire's going," Herbert announced at last. He was so pleased with himself he gave Maudie an amiable whack on the rear. "Come on, old girl. Get going and cut some bread."

Maudie put her hand to her forehead and began to sway gently. Crawford pulled out a chair and pushed her into it.

"You faint just once more," he said callously, "and nobody will take the trouble to pick you up."

"Oh, you brute!" Maudie said.

"Faugh," said Crawford. "If one of you female cripples will hand me a knife, I'll cut the bread. And I'll make the toast too."

"My hero," Isobel breathed. She placed a jar of marmalade gently in his hands. "You can shoot the top off this. Won't that be fun?"

"Gee, yes," Crawford said.

Meanwhile Mrs. Vista had discovered that the next room was a dining room. She sat herself down at the head of the table and instructed Isobel, Joyce and Paula in the fine art of setting a table. From the kitchen came the odor of charred bread and the sound of Crawford's soft but expert cursing.

Eventually Mr. Hunter appeared in the doorway with a plateful of buttered toast and behind him came Herbert bearing an enormous soup tureen full of canned macaroni and cheese.

Chad was sent upstairs to get Gracie. Gracie refused to come down without Miss Rudd because Miss Rudd was hungry again. They came into the dining room arm in arm. Miss Rudd seated herself with dignity beside Mrs. Vista, Gracie sat beside her, Chad slunk into the chair next to Paula, and breakfast began.

Almost immediately Miss Rudd started to enliven what wouldn't have been a dull meal anyway. She accomplished this by the simple but effective method of counting the pieces of toast each one ate. Her eyes followed the plate avidly around the table.

"Four. Two. Two. Five! Goodness, that thin one has had *five*."

Maudie swallowed and protested almost simultaneously. "I have not! I've had four. I have to eat something, don't I?"

"Pay no attention, Maudie angel," Herbert said.

"Five," said Miss Rudd. "*What* a glutton!"

Whenever the plate was passed to her she took a piece, smelled it, and tucked it carefully inside her shawl.

Isobel made several attempts to start polite conversation, but Miss Rudd's personality dominated the room. Hearing Mr. Hunter tell Isobel that Joyce was nineteen, Miss Rudd chuckled gleefully.

"Nineteen," she said. "That thin one's had nineteen. Oh, the glutton!"

"Does she have to sit at the table with us?" Maudie asked desperately.

"Well, it's her table," Gracie said. "It's also her food."

"It's also her food," said Miss Rudd.

She was getting bored, however, and soon she darted to the door, clutching the toast underneath her shawl, and disappeared down the hall.

"She's just gone to hide it," Gracie said easily. "I never saw anybody like it for hiding things."

A meager light began to seep through the high narrow windows. The snow had stopped and the wind had died down again and Crawford prophesied a bright cold day ahead.

Herbert, who had been a boy scout in his youth, suggested building a signal fire in the snow. Crawford said it was impossible. Chad said that on the contrary, it was not impossible, it was possible. The conversation was about to get around to clipping again when a shrill laugh floated into the room.

Miss Rudd was evidently very amused, for the laughter kept on and on until even Gracie began to get uneasy.

"I'd better go and see what she's doing," Gracie said, and left the table.

She found Miss Rudd in the library. She was standing on a chair beside the window and looking out into the snow. Her whole body was shaking with mirth and pieces of toast fell out and scattered on the floor.

"Now, Frances," Gracie said. "Come off that chair and behave yourself. You're making too much noise."

Miss Rudd pointed out the window and laughed again.

"Get down then, and let me look," Gracie said.

Miss Rudd obligingly gave up the chair. Gracie climbed up and looked out the window. At first she could see nothing but vast drifts of snow and several bleak trees. She looked around again and then she saw something sticking out of the snow close beside the house.

It was a foot.

Chapter 9

IT WAS A FOOT STICKING RIGIDLY OUT OF THE snow as if it had been flung there during the night and landed with the sole of the shoe uppermost. There was a layer of snow on the sole. Around the foot the snow was depressed but smooth.

Gracie hung on to the window to steady herself. Miss Rudd had stopped laughing and was regarding her with solicitude.

"What's the matter?" Miss Rudd said.

Gracie clung to the window and whispered, "I don't feel so well. There's a—a foot—out there."

"Well, my goodness," said Miss Rudd cheerfully, "it's only Floraine."

"I want to get down from here. Move away." She climbed down from the chair very slowly, with Miss Rudd giving a helping hand.

"*What* a funny color you are," Miss Rudd said.

Gracie said nothing, but walked as fast as she could to the door. Miss Rudd skimmed along behind her.

When they reached the dining room, Gracie paused in the doorway but Miss Rudd gave her a smart push in the small of the back. Gracie let out a scream and stumbled towards the table. An expectant hush fell over the room.

"What's happened?" Isobel said at last, in a cracked voice.

Gracie sank into a chair. In the dim light her face looked pale and shiny.

"I found—she found—a foot."

"A foot? You don't mean a *foot?*"

Miss Rudd hung her head modestly and said, "*I* found it."

Mrs. Vista half-rose from her chair and sank back again with a vast sigh. "Oh, please! Let's have no more of these jokes. Very bad for the nerves. Imagine anyone finding a foot. You mean you found a shoe, don't you, my dear?"

"A shoe with a foot in it," Gracie said shrilly. "It's out in the snow by the window."

"It's Floraine," Miss Rudd said pleasantly. "What's left of her."

Crawford flung back his chair and grabbed her by the shoulder. "Where is she? Come and show me."

Miss Rudd looked up at him. Her eyes were narrow and bright and her breath hissed in and out through her teeth. "Leave me alone, Harry, or I'll slit you. I'll slit you, Harry. I'll slit you . . ."

Crawford was white around the mouth. His hand dropped to his side and he stepped back. Miss Rudd stared at him unblinkingly for a moment, then gathering her shawl tightly around her shoulders she shambled off out of the door. In the silence that followed they could still hear the hiss of her breath until a door closed somewhere along the hall.

Crawford brushed his hand across his forehead. His mouth moved but he couldn't say anything.

"The library," Gracie croaked. "You can see it from the library window."

"It's—*her* foot?" Isobel said.

"Yes."

Crawford turned and went out. Isobel saw that he was shaking all over. She moved her legs to test them but they seemed very weak suddenly, and too feeble to carry her.

Mrs. Vista had been working up a theory to comfort herself. She said firmly, "I'm sure it's all a mistake. You're probably snow-crazy. I think there's such a thing as snow-crazy, and you see mirages, don't you, Anthony? Or am I thinking of the desert?"

No one cared what Mrs. Vista was thinking, for Crawford had come back into the room. His face seemed to have stiffened into an expressionless mask.

"It's Floraine," he said. "We'll have to go and get her."

"Is she—all there?" Isobel whispered.

Crawford looked at her, his eyes ugly. "How should I know? We'll have to shovel our way out. Come on, Ross. Thropple, you'll help?"

Herbert rose, but Maudie clung to him, crying, "Don't leave me! Don't go away!"

"Tie her up," Crawford said. "There'll be shovels down in the cellar."

Chad Ross was already out of the door. Crawford followed him, not even looking around to see whether Herbert was coming or not.

Herbert, red with anger, thrust Maudie back into her chair. "Sit down. Behave yourself."

"I won't!"

"Stay there or I'll smack you," Herbert said through his teeth.

Maudie, her eyes wide, shrank into her chair and began to cry.

The rest waited silently, watching the door into the hall. Soon Chad Ross went past with a shovel. They heard him open the front door. There was a sudden "swish."

Isobel ran out into the hall. The snow had piled against the door during the night and fallen in on the floor. Chad went to work on it thrusting it back out on the veranda.

When Crawford came up from the cellar he said angrily, "Couldn't you be careful? Don't you know how to open a door with snow piled against it?"

Chad leaned on his shovel. "So you do, do you?"

"Please don't quarrel," Isobel said huskily.

"Beat it, lady," Crawford said. "I've seen enough of you for one night."

There was no bantering note in his voice. He sounded threatening. Isobel went hurriedly back into the dining room.

Paula and Joyce were clearing off the table, moving very quickly as if they were glad of something to do. Isobel sat down beside Gracie.

"You shouldn't have let her out," she said. "You'll have to lock her in again."

"I know," Gracie said in a subdued voice.

"Shall we—go and find her?"

"Find her?" Mrs. Vista said. "The thing is to *lose* her. You should have known she was dangerous, Miss Morning."

Gracie looked at her stubbornly. "Why? She's just like my aunt and my aunt never did a thing like this. Sure, she used to cut things and hide them, but she never did anything really harmful like—like . . ."

"Murder," Mr. Goodwin said.

"We don't know what happened," Isobel said curtly. "There's a possibility that it was only an accident. We'll have to wait and find out."

They waited. The room began to get lighter as the sun rose.

Outside, Crawford flung off his coat and tossed it up on the veranda. He worked faster than the others, with a kind of desperate energy as if he might come upon Floraine still alive. But when he came to the depression in the snow and saw the foot, he knew that Floraine hadn't been alive for a long time.

He threw down his shovel and began to scoop away the snow with his hands. Once his hand touched the ankle and he drew back as if he'd touched something very hot instead of frozen flesh.

A shout rose in his throat and died again. He forced himself to take hold of the leg and pull it a little.

She was lying on her back under the snow. Her other leg was under her, her arms stretched out at her sides. Her body didn't look human. It glittered in the sun and snow was stuck over her eyes so they didn't stare, and her open mouth was clogged with snow. Where her flesh showed it gleamed blue-white like a diamond and it felt as cold and hard.

Crawford closed his eyes. He wanted to yell but he didn't. He kept thinking, Crazy, what a crazy way to die, what a crazy way to look when you're dead . . .

He opened his eyes again, but he didn't look at Floraine. He looked up at the narrow balcony running along the second-floor windows. The railing was soft and beautiful, rounded with snow. It winked in the sun and gave no sign that a woman had been flung over its edge and lay underneath, frozen and brittle as an icicle. Some time in the night there had been marks on that railing, marks of a clinging hand or a falling foot, but the snow, inexorable and kind, had smoothed them and blanketed the dead and pillowed the stark trees.

Snow-crazy, Crawford thought. That's what Mrs. Vista

said. If you thought about it, it would get you, softness that
will suffocate, cold purity that will freeze, beauty that will
blind you . . .

He said in a strange voice, as if he were choking and
didn't care:

"Ross. I've found her. Come here."

Chad came shuffling through the drifts. His face was
shiny red and the sun caught his red hair. Against the snow
he looked like a burning man.

He said, "God!" and stopped still and looked at Floraine.

"We'll have to carry her in," Crawford said, still in the
choking voice. "Take her feet."

Chad bent over. "She's hard."

"Frozen."

"Jesus."

"Take her feet," Crawford said again.

"I can't. I can't get hold of them. They're—they're too
stiff and far apart."

"Bend them."

"Jesus, Crawford!"

"We have to get her inside."

"Couldn't we drag her?"

Crawford's eyes burned. "She's going to be carried, if I
have to do it myself."

He put his hands under her armpits and tried to raise
her. The foot that had been sticking up through the snow
struck Chad in the groin and he cursed and let her fall.
The jolt caused the snow to come out of one of her eyes
and it stared up at the sky.

Chad turned away. "For God's sake."

"Rigid," Crawford said hoarsely. "Won't bend. It'll take
three of us."

"Why can't we drag her?"

"Because I say so," Crawford said.

"Because you say so doesn't make it necessary."

Crawford turned and hit him on the chin. It wasn't a hard
blow but Chad staggered and fell back.

"I owed you that," Crawford said.

Chad got up and brushed off the snow from his coat. His
face was pale.

"Now I owe you something," he said. "You want it now?"

"Some day I'm going to slap your ears off."

Herbert came up then and found them standing looking
at each other. He didn't see Floraine at all until he stumbled
over her foot. He let out a shriek and tripped and fell on

his face in the snow. He came up spluttering and wiping his
eyes.

Crawford said, "Get up and grab one of her legs. We're
going to carry her in."

Crawford's tone was menacing. Herbert touched the leg.

Chad said, "Killer Crawford," in a half-jeering way but
he too moved towards Floraine. He picked up her other leg.
Crawford held her under the armpits and they went forward
drunkenly through the drifts. Both Chad and Crawford swore
audibly, but Herbert was silent. He had his eyes closed and
he wasn't really carrying the frozen leg at all, he held it and
let it lead him along.

When they reached the front door they had to prop her
up so she'd go through. Lying in the hall which was still
dim she seemed to glow like phosphorus and she looked
more terrible, more unreal, than she had outside in the snow.

Crawford took out his handkerchief and tried to brush
off her face, but he saw that the snow wouldn't come off
yet, so he removed his coat and covered the body. One leg
and the hands weren't covered and Chad took off his coat
too and hung it over the leg that still stuck up in the air.
But everything they did only made it more grotesque and
the upstretched leg looked like a clothes prop.

Herbert made a funny noise in the back of his throat
and walked away quickly.

"We can't leave her here like that," Chad said.

"Have to, until she thaws," Crawford said. "The other
doors are narrower and she barely got through the front
door."

"I wouldn't want the women to see her."

"Let them look the other way. Or keep them in the dining
room. Who in hell cares?"

"I like your mood," Chad said. "It just suits you."

Crawford didn't answer or even turn around. He was looking down at Floraine with a sad, tired expression in his eyes.

Chad shrugged and went into the dining room. When
Crawford heard the door shut he bent down and took the
coats off Floraine.

She was wearing a dark blue coat over her white uniform.
None of her clothes were torn, and there were no bloodstains
visible. He looked at her neck and her fingernails and the
pupils of her eyes, but there was nothing to show how
Floraine had died.

She may actually have frozen to death, Crawford thought,
or suffocated in the snow.

What was she doing on the balcony dressed in her coat?

Whose window was above where the body had been found?

Behind him he heard the dining-room door open again. He turned quickly and shouted, "Stay in there!"

But Isobel was already in the hall, and she had already seen Floraine. Her eyes were glassy and she had one hand to her throat.

"Can't you—cover her—up?" she whispered.

"I did cover her up," Crawford said dryly. "She looks like hell anyway. Now how would you like to go back in that room and stay there?"

She seemed ready to cry. "I thought I—I could do something."

"She's dead as a doornail, sister, and you can't do a thing. Listen." He drew his foot back and gave one of Floraine's legs a little kick. It sounded as though he had kicked a piece of stone.

Isobel stepped back, staring at him. "Must you be so— brutal?"

Crawford laughed and said, "Brutal, for Christ's sake. Listen, sister, I'm nervous." He began to walk towards her very slowly. "When I'm nervous I do anything. I've got to have action when I'm nervous. You go back into that dining room and tell the gentlemen to step out into the hall two at a time and I'll knock their heads together."

He was within two feet of her now and there was a crazy light in his eyes.

"I won't hurt you," he added softly. "I like the shape of your mouth and the way your eyebrows grow and your chin . . ." He put his hand under her chin and raised her face. His hand was not gentle, and his mouth when he put it over hers was hard and cold.

She stood motionless, hardly breathing, hypnotized by this strange man who kissed her as if he hated her. Finally he drew away and she saw that he was smiling a little, though his jaw was clenched.

"That's not what I mean by action," he said. "But failing anything better . . ." He shrugged his shoulders and turned and walked away, back to Floraine.

Isobel put her hand slowly to her mouth and rubbed it. Her legs were trembling and she felt cold all over as if his cold mouth had chilled her.

"Don't stand there," he said sharply.

His tone whipped the blood into her face. "Don't order me around."

"No?"

"And don't touch me again."

"You're safe. I'd rather kiss an ice-cube."

There was a silence. Then Isobel said quietly. "Was Floraine murdered?"

Her quietness affected him. "She was," he said more civilly.

"How?"

"I don't know. No marks on her. She was pushed off the balcony and may have smothered in the snow."

"Then if we'd looked for her right away . . ."

"Shut up," he said savagely. He drew in his breath painfully. "You're blaming me?"

"No, no, I'm not. All of us . . ."

"No, I'm to blame. I was sure she was hiding somewhere. I never thought of looking outside. She might have still been alive while we were shoveling that coal looking for her body. And all the time she was out there fresh-frozen like a Birds Eye chicken."

"Don't talk like that," Isobel said faintly.

"Where's Miss Rudd now?"

' "Gracie Morning is looking for her upstairs."

"Miss Morning is a brave woman," Crawford said. "Or is she stupid? Or—" he smiled dryly— "does she know more than the rest of us about Floraine's death? Does she know, for instance, that Miss Rudd didn't murder Floraine?"

"You're wrong about Gracie. She just doesn't seem to realize—she's irresponsible."

"I wonder how irresponsible," Crawford said.

"You're wrong," Isobel repeated dully. "You've forgotten the cat. Miss Rudd killed the cat. And what happened to M. Hearst, the bus-driver?"

"Would Floraine go for a walk on the balcony with Miss Rudd? Look again and you'll see she has a coat on."

Isobel looked again and as she looked one of Floraine's hands moved. She turned and ran. She heard Crawford laughing behind her and his sharp brittle voice saying, "She's *thawing*, sister. She's just *thawing*."

Chapter 10

MAURICE HEARST OPENED HIS EYES. A SLIVER OF sun shot through a crack in the drawn blind and hit his eyeballs. He felt a sharp searing pain go right through his head.

He closed his eyes, wincing, and thought, funny, I don't remember that crack in the blind. It wasn't there before.

He turned his head and burrowed it into the pillow to shut out the light and the sounds that came from the next room, and from the street. But the sounds kept coming right through the pillow, and he could still imagine the sliver of light and it was almost as bad as seeing it, because it worried him. He couldn't remember the crack in the blind, but he didn't want to get up and look at it, he didn't want to move at all. His head was too hot and heavy a thing to go carrying around. And it must be early, his alarm hadn't gone off yet.

But as soon as he thought of his alarm this began to worry him too. Maybe he'd forgotten to wind it, or the clock had stopped. It wasn't a very good clock anyway, it had a loud rattling alarm and the tick was wheezy and uneven and you could hear it when you were walking down the hall even before you opened the door.

He moved his head and listened and heard no ticking, nothing but the boom-thump of his own blood pounding in his ears. He forced himself to open his eyes again. Then he lay on his back and looked at the ceiling and tried to concentrate.

The blind and the clock—and now the ceiling. It wasn't the right color.

"God," he said aloud, and put up his hand to brush away the sudden sweat from his forehead. He saw his wrist, thick and tanned, with coarse fair hairs on it. But it was a swell wrist, he could remember it, it was his.

His eye traveled up and he saw that he was wearing his coat. He had gone to sleep with his clothes on. He had never done that before, never been that drunk.

He moved again and the armholes of the coat felt tight and uncomfortable and the sleeves were too short.

Breathing hard and fighting off nausea, he sat up in the bed. These weren't his clothes, this wasn't his bed or his room, there was no clock . . .

No, that couldn't be right.

I'm sick, he thought, I'm very, very sick and I'm imagining things and in a minute everything will be all right. When this pain goes away, when I can see better, it will be my room again.

He waited, his eyes closed, trying to force himself to breathe deeply and evenly. But he didn't get enough oxygen that way, and he had to open his mouth and gasp and drag the air into his lungs.

Last night. Remember last night. Think about last night. Get that straight first.

But it wouldn't come. Last night seemed ordinary. All his nights were pretty much the same. He played poker with Gaston, the headwaiter, and a couple of kitchen boys, or he went to bed early and read a book, or he took on some of the guests for billiards in the basement. Nobody could beat him at billiards. He had a steady eye and good nerves. . . .

"Good nerves," he said aloud, and tried to laugh about it. But the laugh turned out to be a whimper and his voice sounded as strange to him as the room and the bed and the clothes. It was weak and husky.

I'm sick, he thought again. Where did I get sick? Where was I? Where am I?

He looked around the room again. It wasn't his room, but he'd seen it before. Somewhere, sometime before he had been in this room.

There was a pitcher of water on the little table beside the bed and three glasses.

Three glasses. Why three glasses? He squinted to make his eyes focus better, but there were still three glasses. He picked one up and poured some water into it. He was very thirsty and in a minute all the water was gone from the pitcher and he was feeling steadier and the pain behind his eyes had settled down into a gnawing ache. When he put the glass back on the table he saw an empty quart bottle of gin on the floor.

Gin, he thought, I never drink gin.

But the bottle was empty, and he, obviously, had been full, so he must have drunk gin, or else he'd had someone with him.

As soon as he thought of that he knew it was right. He couldn't remember anybody, but something seemed to move in his mind and click into place. Someone had come here with him, maybe two people if there were three glasses.

From the next room came the sound of a vacuum cleaner starting up. I'm in a hotel, he thought. If I could get over to the window and pull up the blind and look out maybe I'd know where I am. I could always remember roads and buildings. . . .

Roads.

There was something about the word that hit him. His

heart began to thump again and the blood roared in his ears. *Roads.*

He swung his legs off the bed and staggered over to the window and tore at the blind to get it up. It came off the roller and fell on his head and he fought it off desperately as if it were an animate thing, and a mortal enemy.

It ripped and fell to the floor and he looked down at it savagely and kicked it away with his foot.

The sun beat in on his eyes and for a second he could see nothing but a black-red glare. The glare faded and became the orange twinkle of sun on snow.

He was on the second floor of the hotel. Just outside his window a painted sign swung gently back and forth: Hotel Metropole, it said on one side. Prix modérés. Tout confort. On the other side it said, Metropole Hotel. All Conveniences. Reasonable Rates.

The sign brought everything back so vividly that he had to breathe deeply again to ward off the sudden nausea that hit him.

The bus. Where's the bus? I've lost the bus.

He strained his eyes to see across the street. There was the station looking the way it always did, too bright and modern in this sleepy third-rate little town. But the place in front of the station where he always parked the bus was empty.

That was where he kept the bus, waiting for the Montreal train to come in. Sometimes it was late and he went across to the Metropole for coffee or beer, but he'd never stayed here before. He'd never been upstairs.

He turned away from the window and sat on the bed holding his head in his hands and trying to think through the pain. Maybe if I talked out loud, he thought, maybe if I asked myself questions I'd remember everything.

What's your name?

Maurice A. Hearst. A for Albert.

How old are you?

Twenty-six, hell, no, twenty-seven. Who cares? Old enough to know better than to talk to strangers.

Strangers, eh? What kind of strangers?

I don't know. That just slipped out. I don't . . .

Well, take it easy. Where do you work?

I work for the Chateau Neige. I drive their bus. I've been there for two years now and I'm a damn good driver and that bus gets through roads that nothing else can get through but a snow plow. It's like a jeep, see? It bounces. It doesn't look so hot and you have to coddle the engine but . . .

All right, all right, so it's a jeep. Where were you last night?

I don't know.

All right. Where were you this morning?

Here.

You couldn't have been here this morning. You drove the bus down this morning, didn't you? That was this morning, wasn't it? Wasn't it? *Wasn't it?*

He groaned, "Oh, Jesus," and rolled his head back and forth. Then he began again.

You still there, Mr. Hearst?

Sure, sure. It's my wrist, isn't it? Sure, I'm here.

You know what day this is?

No.

You know what time it is?

No—wait, the sun—it's noon, twelve o'clock.

Good work, Mr. Hearst. Where are you usually at noon?

I'm in my bus waiting for the train to come in.

So that makes this today and not yesterday. Isn't that right?

Sure, sure. It's today. If it isn't yesterday it must be today.

So you've lost twenty-four hours. Where were you yesterday at noon?

I was in my bus. I had the motor idling because on the trip down it coughed a couple of times and I didn't want to have any trouble with it going back. It was ten below and the roads were as bad as I've ever seen them.

Anybody with you on the trip down?

No, not this time.

All right. You're sitting with the motor idling. Do you remember seeing anyone?

Sure, a kid with a St. Bernard.

That's dandy. Maybe *he* got you drunk.

I wasn't drunk. I was knocked out or something. I'm sick.

All right. The kid and the dog. And what else?

A couple of guys came out of the station. I remember thinking it was funny because the older guy was all dressed up but the younger one was shabby. . . .

Hearst got off the bed and walked over to the window again. He tried to picture the bus standing in front of the station, and himself behind the wheel, and the two men walking out of the station. There had been no sun and the wind ripped up the street, and the train was going to be late. . . . The two men came over and one of them rapped on the door of the bus, it was the well-dressed one who looked as if he came from the city. . . .

Hearst looked down at the blue serge suit he was wearing. It belonged to the shabby young man, the one who hadn't talked. The older man had done the talking. He looked as if he came from the city. . . .

"Is this the Chateau Neige bus?"

"Sure is," Hearst said.

"How long do you wait here?"

"As long as it takes the train to come in. Been late a lot the last month."

The older man grinned and said, "The war or the weather?"

"Both," Hearst said. He liked talking but the two men were keeping the door open and the bus heater didn't work so well. He said, "You want to go up to the Lodge? Well, hop in. I have to close this door."

"No, no," the older man said. "I'm supposed to meet somebody here, a lady. She's going on up but I've got to wait a couple of days in town here. Business. Any place I can get a drink?"

Hearst pointed. "Sure. The Metropole."

The shabby man smiled and nodded his head.

"Maybe you'd like to join us?" the older man suggested. "We're strangers in town . . ."

"Have to wait here," Hearst said, but the idea tempted him. He'd go and look on the call board and see how late the train was going to be and maybe he'd have time for a quick one.

Both of the men looked pleased, and they went with him to see about the train. It wasn't due for half an hour.

The older man said his name was Aldington. He was in the lumber business. The other man, hunched inside his coat even in the bar, kept smiling stupidly at everybody and didn't say anything.

Hearst ordered beer but Mr. Aldington wanted whisky and after a whispered conversation with the bartender and the passing of a bill, he got it.

"Too cold for beer," he said to Hearst. "What's this place like, to stay at, I mean?"

Hearst didn't know. He noticed that Mr. Aldington was carrying a brief-case.

Mr. Aldington saw him looking at it and winked. "Stimulant," he said. "I always freeze in this country."

He went over to the desk and registered. When he came back he said he wanted to go upstairs and deposit his brief-case. Did Mr. Hearst want to come too, and they'd all have a drink and then go back to the station together?

It *was* too cold for beer, Hearst decided, and if Mr. Aldington was going to come up to the Lodge later to see his girl friend, it would be better to humor him . . .

The last he saw of Mr. Aldington, Mr. Aldington was disappearing in a gray fuzzy blur which finally wavered and dissolved into nothing.

Hearst looked around the room and found that they'd left him a coat and a peaked cap and a pair of heavy work boots. He put them on and went downstairs, hanging onto the railing. He walked drunkenly over to the desk and the Frenchwoman who owned the Metropole looked up in surprise. She didn't recognize him at first.

Then she said, "Why, Monsieur Hearst!"

"What day is this?" Hearst croaked, swaying on his feet.

"Drunk," said Madame Picard sadly. "This is Friday. I did not see you enter."

"Where's Henri?" Henri was the bartender.

"This is Henri's holiday," Madame Picard said. "And I would not allow him to serve you in your condition. A man who must drive a bus, a man who is responsible for the lives and safety of . . ."

"I've been here all night."

"Then you owe me money," Madame Picard said and promptly opened her registry book. "There is no record, Monsieur Hearst. You are imagining things. Monsieur Picard, who had his weakness like every man, used to imagine that there were . . ."

"I'm not drunk," Hearst said.

"Ho, ho," said Madame Picard gaily. "Monsieur Picard to the life! Never, never drunk, until he fell over!"

Hearst lurched to the door and wrenched it open, and gasped the cold air into his lungs. Then he closed the door behind him and began to run.

The station-master was in his office. When he saw Hearst he regarded him with a frown.

"It's about time," he said. "Train's been in ten minutes and there's a gang of weekenders raising a racket for the bus."

He pointed to a group of young men and women standing together in one corner, talking loudly.

"I haven't got the bus," Hearst said. "Someone stole it yesterday."

"You're crazy," the station-master said. "Where's your uniform? What are you doing in that rig?"

"I'm telling you," Hearst said wildly. "A couple of men

took the bus yesterday and left me doped up in the Metropole all night."

"Some kidder you are," the station-master said sourly. "I saw you leave here yesterday. Had a loadful, too, the kind that pay high and like it. And you phoned in like you usually do from Chapelle when the weather's bad. You said you could make it all right but the roads were bad and you'd be late."

"I phoned in?" Hearst said slowly. Mr. Aldington knew his job, whatever it was. Only someone who'd made the trip before could have known that he phoned in from Chapelle when the going was tough.

"Give me the phone," he said. "I've got to get in touch with the Lodge."

"Well, you'd better use pigeons," the station-master said acidly. "The wires are down. I just tried them, to see what was keeping you."

Hearst sat down abruptly in a chair and passed his hand over his eyes. The station-master watched him with a worried frown.

"No one else but you could get that bus through the roads the way they were yesterday," he said.

"I know," Hearst said, with mournful pride. "And what did they want with it? Who in hell would want *my bus?*"

"Kidnapping, maybe. You'd better phone the police."

Five minutes later Sergeant Mackay of the Mounted Police arrived at the station. A big, taciturn, weather-beaten man of forty, he listened carefully to Hearst's story. He knew Hearst as a steady young man who liked his job and drank very little. Every day Hearst's bus passed the corner where the courthouse was and Mackay often waved to him from his office window. He had waved yesterday. He remembered noticing that the bus was full and wondering what strange urge brought people with money to this wilderness in order to slide down hills and break their necks.

"Sounds a little crazy," he said when Hearst had finished.

"Crazy as hell," Hearst said wearily. "What did they want —the bus or the people in it or just one of the people in it? *And where are the people now?*"

"Frozen to death," said the station-master in a sinister whisper.

"Keep out of this, George," Mackay said, and turned back to Hearst. "They may have gotten the bus through all right. We've had no complaints from the Lodge."

"The wires are down," Hearst said. "And I guess they

figured I just stayed in town on account of the roads. I had to do that once last winter."

Mackay took out his notebook. He used the notebook chiefly for grocery lists provided by his wife. There wasn't much crime in the winter up here. People were too busy trying to keep warm.

"What did these two men look like?" he said. "Were they French or English?"

"The big one, Aldington, was English, I think. He had on a gray felt hat and a gray overcoat that looked expensive. Dark skin, black hair, and a lot of teeth."

"What do you mean, a lot of teeth?" said the stationmaster.

Mackay said, "George, you got work to do, do it. Tell that gang over there that there isn't any bus today. They'll have to stay at the hotel overnight." George went away reluctantly.

"He was toothy," Hearst said.

"Age?"

"I don't know. Maybe forty, maybe thirty-five. He looked fit, though, and pretty muscular. His eyes were brown, I guess, and he was good-looking."

"And the other guy?"

Hearst looked helpless. "I don't know. He didn't talk. He just smiled and seemed kind of half-witted. I figure he was French and didn't want to be spotted."

"He didn't make any noise?"

"Well, he laughed once. It was a crazy laugh, sort of high and giggly and shrill. Sounded like Hitler."

"Like Hitler," Mackay said thoughtfully, and stared across the desk at Hearst. "Go on."

"He looked as if he'd been outdoors a lot. He had on these clothes I'm wearing so I guess he was a little smaller than me."

Mackay ran his eye slowly over the blue serge suit, the peaked cap and the overcoat.

He said suddenly, "Let me see those shoes. Take them off."

Hearst took them off and Mackay examined the shoes and the lining. Then he dived for the Montreal and District telephone directory. Hearst peered over his shoulder and noted the page number and saw where Mackay's finger stopped on the page.

Mackay said, "Step out there a minute, Hearst. I'm calling long distance on *business*."

"Can't I . . .?"

"No."

Hearst, minus shoes, walked over to the main door where the station-master was giving the weekenders a long and untruthful account of the missing bus. He told them that the drifts were fifteen feet high, that even the snow plow was stuck, and that the Metropole was one of the finest hotels in the country. They would be, he said, very surprised.

They certainly will, Hearst thought, watching them troop across the street.

"You're some liar," he said.

"Sure," George said. "But look at my results. They're happy as hell because they got something to tell their friends when they get back."

Mackay came to the door. He handed Hearst the boots. "I'm going back to the office. Everything's settled. I've got someone tracing the bus and I know who one of your two friends is."

He smiled and walked out.

"Hey," Hearst shouted, but the door had closed again.

"How do you like that?" George said. "No gratitude in him. Wouldn't even give us a clue."

He took one of the boots and examined it but it seemed an ordinary boot. He tossed it back to Hearst who put it on. They went back to the office.

Hearst picked up the telephone directory and turned to the page Mackay had been looking at. At the approximate place where Mackay's finger had stopped were three private numbers and the number of a boys' reform school.

"For God's sake," Hearst said in disgust. "A reform school!"

"What's that?" George said quickly, and Hearst told him. "It's a clue!" George yelped. "Oh boy, a clue!"

"A clue, hell," Hearst said. "If either of those guys came from a boy's reform school I should be in diapers."

Chapter 11

"MY HEART," SAID MRS. VISTA, "IS NOT WHAT IT used to be. I feel I must have a cup of good strong tea."

Mrs. Vista's heart had never been what it used to be and

this announcement failed to electrify anyone. Only Joyce Hunter bothered to reply, and then it was the kind of reply that Mrs. Vista found most unsatisfactory.

"If you want some tea," Joyce said moodily, "make it yourself."

Mrs. Vista, still seated at the head of the dining-room table, surveyed her regally.

"You are a rude young snippet."

"I don't know what a snippet is," Joyce said coldly.

"You don't have to know, you *are* one."

"Well, if I'm a snippet, you're a—a paramour."

"A paramour!" Mrs. Vista clapped a hand to her heart and made a little bleating noise. This forced Maudie to make a little bleating noise too, since she had her status as invalid of the party to maintain. The competition was getting lively when Isobel precipitated herself into the room and slammed the door violently behind her.

Chad Ross said, "I told you you shouldn't go out. We'll all have to stay here until she's moved into the library."

Mr. Hunter rose from the table and helped Isobel to a chair. Then he sat down beside her and patted her hand and made soothing sounds of sympathy.

"Was it terrible?" he whispered.

She nodded, half-angrily, and took her hand away. "They're all taking it so—so calmly. No, not calmly, but as if they don't care what's happened."

"Why should we?" Mr. Hunter said in surprise.

"But she's dead—murdered! Don't you feel anything at all?"

"It's a pity, of course, but I barely knew the woman, and one can't expect total strangers . . ."

"But if you saw her!"

"Precisely," said Mr. Hunter dryly, "why I don't want to see her. It's not unlikely that you're the one who is wrong. You are making the worst of a bad situation by allowing yourself to become emotional about something you can't do anything about."

He coughed primly and stroked his mustache. "It is far, far better to spend one's emotions on oneself, like Mrs. Vista and Mrs. Thropple, or not to have any emotions, like Joyce."

"Or to close your eyes, like Mr. Hunter," Isobel added.

Mr. Hunter smiled benignly and said nothing.

"And I *can* do something about the situation," Isobel said. "Perhaps you'd like to come into the library with me?"

"No, no thanks. I am happier here. What do you want in the library?"

"There's a book there I'd like to see. It's on local geography and we might be able to figure out exactly where we are and do something about it."

"I prefer to wait for the rescuers," Mr. Hunter said blandly.

Isobel glanced at her watch. "It's ten o'clock. The rescuers are taking their time, aren't they?"

Mr. Hunter was beginning to be annoyed. "Kindly lower your voice. You wouldn't like to put the women in hysterics, would you?"

"I'd *love* it," Isobel said through her teeth.

"You're a very odd woman," Mr. Hunter said. She had gotten up from the chair and was looking down at him with contempt. "I earnestly advise you to stay in here with the rest of us."

"Your daughter has more spunk than you have," Isobel said witheringly.

"I'm sure of it," Mr. Hunter replied with sorrow. He watched Isobel move towards the door. There was a noticeable reluctance in her step, but once the door was opened she swung out into the hall, almost gaily.

She felt better in the hall, even with Floraine there, even with Crawford in a savage mood.

The others, encased in their four stone walls of indifference, irritated her. They aren't *human,* she thought, except Gracie and Miss Rudd and maybe Crawford. Even Paula Lashley, who seemed like a nice girl, could not disentangle herself from her own mesh of problems long enough to act human.

"You back again?" Crawford said. He had propped a kitchen chair against one wall and was leaning back, with the bottle of brandy in one hand. Isobel saw with a shock that the brandy was nearly half gone and that Crawford was actually smiling.

Crawford noticed her glance. "I am quietly getting a snootful, Isobel. I'd ask you to join me but I have already drunk from the bottle and I don't approve of women drinking. Cuts down my supply."

Isobel edged along the opposite wall, carefully avoiding Floraine's body.

"Where are you going, Isobel?"

"To the library," Isobel said coldly.

"For a good book to read. I agree, there's nothing like a

good book when you find yourself cooped up with one, maybe two, homicidal maniacs, and a cold-storage corpse."

"Getting drunk isn't going to help."

"Sure it's going to help, it's going to help *me*. The rest don't matter."

"A very refreshing viewpoint," Isobel said and turned her back on him. But she didn't hurry into the library.

"Except possibly," Crawford added thoughtfully, "you. You may matter. I shall try to find out."

"Don't bother."

"No bother at all," Crawford said graciously, and took another drink. "I have always had difficulty with my women. I think the reason is that I've never done enough reconnoitering. Take a gun, for instance. When you buy a gun you don't go into a store and pick out one because it has such a cute little trigger. No ma'am. You scout around first."

"Thanks," Isobel said. "I'll remember that."

"Do."

"By the way, where is your gun?"

"Here." He patted his pocket. "Snug as a bug."

"What's your real name?"

He grinned and looked at her owlishly. "Now, Isobel. You're plying me with liquor to make me talk. I won't talk, Isobel, but you may have my card. Have a bunch of them, take them home to your friends."

He tossed some cards across to her. She stooped and picked them up. The first one said, "M. R. MacTavish, Insurance Adjustor." The others included an Oriental Rug Dealer called Marink, a Mr. Kelly who ran a Finance Company, and a Mr. Hugh Henderson whose business was not stated.

Isobel let the cards fall to the floor. She said dryly, "A man of many moods, apparently."

"That's me," Crawford said. "Never a dull moment. And think of it—if you marry me you can pick your own name. Not many women have such a glowing opportunity. Which name do you like best?"

"I'll have to think it over," Isobel said.

"Pick any one you like," Crawford said with a vague sweep of his hand.

Isobel gave the cards a kick and walked rapidly into the library. Her face was flushed and she felt warm and a little shocked at herself because Crawford had made her forget Floraine.

She sat down in one of the sheet-covered chairs and thought about Crawford-Kelly-Marink-Henderson-MacTavish.

After a time her face cooled, and she noticed that the room was very cold and thought suddenly about the furnace. No one had tended the furnace.

She rushed out and told Crawford. Crawford said he personally felt very warm but if Isobel would like to fix the furnace he offered no objections.

"Why should I have to fix it?" Isobel cried. "The house is practically swarming with able-bodied men and I have to do everything! It's not fair."

"I know it isn't," Crawford said and took a gulp of brandy. "It's a damn shame. But it's life," he added sadly, and waved her away.

She strode angrily down the hall and flung open the door into the kitchen. She found Mrs. Vista trying to make herself some tea on the stove, but she swept past her without speaking and hurled herself down the cellar steps.

"Really," said Mrs. Vista pensively, "how very strange everyone else is."

Isobel opened the heavy door that led into the furnace room. She expected a gust of warm air to meet her, but instead there seemed to be a very cold draught sweeping across at her and the cellar was quite bright.

She looked and saw that the door at the head of the short stairway leading outside was open.

There was a man standing in the doorway. He was watching her, motionless, as if he had frozen there.

Isobel took a step back. Neither of them spoke. The man, outlined by sun, seemed enormous and sinister. He was dressed in skiing clothes and he still had his poles strapped to his wrists. He moved suddenly and leaned against the door as if he were unutterably weary. One of the poles slipped off his wrist and clattered down the steps.

The man stared at it a moment, then he began to lumber down the steps after it, hanging on to the wall.

"I'm—I'm lost," he said huskily and fell on his knees. Crouching there, he looked up at her with wild eyes.

Dazed with shock she didn't move forward to help him.

"Don't be frightened," he said, trying to smile. "I'm cold. I can't move very well. Close the door."

She went automatically up the steps and closed the door. With the sun shut out the cellar was dim.

"Now come down here again," the man said, and even though his voice was feeble and he was too ill to stand up, he had authority. She recognized it and came down the steps and stood a few feet away from him, like a child awaiting instructions from an adult.

She saw that he had a very dark skin and black eyes and she knew he was a French-Canadian from his intonations. He wasn't as tall as she had thought, and a great deal of his bulk was clothing, layers and layers of it.

He began to take it off, holding out his arm to her when he needed help.

"Fingers numb," he said. "Been out—a long time."

She pulled his heavy jacket off. She saw him staring at her clothes.

"You live here?" he said.

"No." She hesitated, wondering how to explain the whole crazy chain of events to a stranger. "No, we're lost too. There are quite a few of us here."

"Who owns the house?"

"A Miss Rudd," Isobel said. "She's—she stayed here with her nurse."

"Sick?"

"No . . . No, she's a little peculiar," Isobel said and began to giggle. The man just stared at her and waited until she had stopped.

"I'm sorry," Isobel said in a muffled voice. "I guess I've had—too much excitement."

"Yes?" He had a sharp alert voice. "What kind?"

"Miss Rudd, and the cat and—and everything. You'd better stay down here in the cellar for a while and I'll bring you some food and blankets."

"Yes? Why? Why should I stay here?"

"There's something in the hall you'd better not see. I mean, I'll explain everything later . . ."

He put his hand gently on her wrist. "No. Now."

"It's—a—a—body."

"In the hall? A body?" He smiled slightly. "You're not Miss Rudd yourself, are you?"

She turned her head away. "No. Miss Rudd killed her nurse."

She felt his recoil and thought, he thinks I'm crazy. She said, "I didn't want to tell you now. You made me tell you. I know how incredible it sounds."

"I'm sure you don't," he said grimly. "You're not making this up to get rid of me, are you?"

"I'll go upstairs and bring you something . . ."

"No, wait."

She paused at the door and looked back. He was standing up again gazing at her warily.

"I'll come with you," he said.

"No. I'll have to tell the others you're here. They've had
so many surprises and one of the women faints . . ."

He brushed her words away with a gesture.

"I'll come with you," he said again and walked toward
her, limping on one foot. When they came to the stairs he
said, "Go up first."

"No . . ."

"Go up first. I want you in front of me."

"I'm not crazy."

"Neither am I," he said. "That's why I want you in front
of me."

"How dare you order me around like this?" she said
shrilly. "How *dare* you think I'm—I'm crazy!"

In the kitchen Mrs. Vista said with a sigh: "Miss Seton
appears to be shouting about something. Shall we ignore
her?"

"Yes. Quite," said Mr. Goodwin.

"I agree. *So* much better in the long run. Tea, Anthony?"

Mr. Goodwin took his cup and settled down beside the
stove. The door from the cellar opened and Isobel Seton
emerged slowly. Her face was white and her hair was wispy
and she looked at Mr. Goodwin with glassy eyes.

"Look what I found," she said in a low voice.

"You found something?" Mr. Goodwin said. "Well, well."

He stared with his mouth open as Isobel proceeded
through the kitchen, followed by the limping man. They
went out into the hall and the man turned and shut the door
again carefully. He had barely glanced at Mrs. Vista and
Mr. Goodwin.

"Extraordinary," said Mr. Goodwin hollowly.

"Most unconventional," Mrs. Vista agreed.

"Makes one doubt the senses, don't you think?"

"You're quite right," Mrs. Vista said thoughtfully. "And
once one doubts the senses what is there left for one?"

"Nothing," said Mr. Goodwin, and sipped his tea.

Outside the door the man had stopped and grabbed Isobel's hand.

He said, "This is the hall, is it?"

Isobel nodded wordlessly.

"Do you see any body?"

"No," Isobel said in a strangled whisper.

"Did you ever see it?"

"It was there. Someone must have—taken it away."

"What is this game?" the man said quietly. "If you simply
want to get rid of me I'll be delighted to leave. Have I
accidentally stumbled on an insane asylum?"

"Mr. Crawford must have put the body some place. He was waiting for it to thaw."

"To *what?*"

"Thaw. It was frozen."

The man stared at her a moment, his face strained and puzzled.

"Madame," he said, "you were correct. The cellar's the place for me. I shall stay long enough to get warm. And don't bother coming with me. I can find my way."

He turned.

"You imbecile!" Isobel hissed. "Can't you see the water on the floor? That's where she was lying. Mr. Crawford was just waiting for her to . . ."

"*Thaw.*" Crawford's voice whipped down the hall. He was standing in the library doorway, still holding the brandy bottle.

There was a sudden screaming silence, then Crawford's voice again, calm and dry:

"Isobel, you're being true to me yet? Or can't you help yourself?"

The man coughed and said, "Sir, I am sorry to disturb you but I was lost and came upon this house. I think my foot is partially frozen."

In spite of his words there was the same air of authority about him that Isobel had found disconcerting. He didn't sound sorry, but challenging, and his intense gaze, fixed on Crawford, was half-puzzled, half-insolent.

Crawford began to walk towards them. He wore the ugly little smile that was now familiar to Isobel, and his eyelids were flickering.

"Yeah?" he said. "Your foot's frozen?"

"Yes, I think so."

"What do you want me to do, amputate it?"

"No, that won't be necessary," the man said coolly. "All I require is some food and shelter for a time. You seem to be a stranger in these parts. No doubt you are unfamiliar with the laws of French-Canadian hospitality."

Isobel didn't like the way they were looking at each other. She said hastily, "Of course. I'll see about the food . . ."

Crawford's voice cut in. "Is that a fact? Maybe I'm not interested in the laws of French-Canadian hospitality. Maybe I don't care if your foot falls off at the hip."

"I do, however." The man held out his hand to Crawford. "My name is Dubois, René Dubois. Perhaps you have heard of me?"

Crawford took the hand but didn't shake it. He looked at it, turning it over as if it were a piece of fish.

"Can't say I have," he said in a bored voice.

The man's eyes were hard and glittering. "You are too old to learn politeness, Monsieur, but not too young to see that it is sometimes necessary to feign it. I am feigning it. Be so good as to do the same."

Crawford said nothing, but he looked sulky.

"Who are you?" Isobel said quickly.

"You are not interested in skiing?" Dubois said, smiling. "I am a cross-country endurance skier. Unfortunately the blizzard caught me yesterday and I was forced to abandon some of my equipment and spend the night in a maple-sugar shed."

Crawford had another lightning mood-change. He said easily, "Don't let this fellow win you away from me with mere words. I, too, can ski."

"Give him the rest of the brandy," Isobel said sharply. "Here, Mr. Dubois. You'd better take off your shoe. Come into the sitting room."

"I rarely drink," Dubois said, "but on this occasion, I think I might."

"I might have known it," Crawford said and handed him the bottle. "On two bottles of this stuff you'll be able to ski in the fourth dimension, but I hope you get all my diseases."

Dubois drank from the bottle. He was completely at ease. Neither Crawford's cracks nor Isobel's fluttering ministrations made a dent in his self-assurance. He followed Isobel into the sitting room and even while he limped his walk had something swaggering about it.

He sat down and took off his one shoe and sock and examined his foot.

"It is not frozen," he said.

"Gee, I'm glad," Crawford said elaborately.

Isobel said, "I didn't put coal on the furnace, Mr. Crawford. Would you oblige?"

"You always win eventually, don't you?" Crawford said sadly and went out.

"He is a strange fellow," Dubois said, tying up his shoe again.

"If you think he's strange, wait until you meet the rest of them."

"I must apologize to you, Madame."

"Isobel Seton."

"Miss Seton, I must apologize for doubting your word."

"That's all right," Isobel said. "I doubt it myself sometimes. Would you prefer to have your food here or go in the dining room with the others?"

"Here," Dubois said, showing a row of glistening white teeth. "I shall feel better able to meet the strange people after I have eaten."

Isobel went back into the kitchen. Mrs. Vista greeted her vaguely.

"My dear, that *was* a man you had with you, wasn't it?"

"It was," Isobel said. "May I gave him some of your tea?"

"A little, perhaps. Where did you find him? Really, how extraordinary going down into a cellar and finding a man. It's never happened to me. But then, I rarely visit cellars."

"This is the first time I have ever found a man in a cellar," Isobel said coldly. "Where is the bread?"

"Over there," Mrs. Vista said, with a sweep of her hand.

Isobel cut bread and buttered it and put some marmalade in a dish while Mrs. Vista followed her about the kitchen. Mrs. Vista said that human adjustments were extraordinary, really. At first she was utterly confused when she saw the man, she confessed, but now she had adjusted to him.

"Frightfully handsome, in a rugged way, wasn't he, Anthony?"

Mr. Goodwin's adjustments came slower, apparently, for he said he didn't remember.

"I think," said Mrs. Vista, "that a new face is just what we required in this house. One tires of the old faces, though I find *mobile* faces less tiring than still faces. I think Anthony has a very mobile face."

Mr. Goodwin obligingly grimaced.

"See, Miss Seton?" Mrs. Vista said. "That's what I mean. *Mobility.* I feel it's everything in a face."

"Oh, I don't know," Isobel said with an appraising glance at Mr. Goodwin. She picked up the dishes and as she passed Mr. Goodwin, she said, "Give it a rest, brother. Nobody's looking at you but God."

She swept out the door and kicked it shut with her foot. I must *not* talk like Crawford, she told herself sternly, I must ignore Crawford, Crawford is a louse.

"Yoo hoo," said a voice from the stairs, and Gracie Morning's face appeared over the banister.

She was looking, Isobel noticed, very pretty and neat. Her hair was a halo of bronze ringlets and her face was freshly made up.

Isobel stopped still.

"Where's Miss Rudd?"

"Miss Rudd?" Gracie said, swinging down the steps. "Oh, yes. Well, I looked for her but she wasn't around so I decided to fix myself up a bit in case we're rescued. I was a wreck, no kidding."

"You mean you didn't even find her?"

"That's what I said," Gracie said pleasantly. "Don't throw a fit. She'll be all right."

"She'll be all right!" Isobel cried. "What about *us?* We thought you had her upstairs, we thought you were keeping her quiet up there!"

"How could I keep her quiet if I couldn't find her?" Gracie asked reasonably.

"You let her out. It's your responsibility to find her again. She's dangerous. Don't you understand?"

"Well, to tell you the truth, I've been thinking it over and I decided that I was right in the first place. She's not dangerous." Gracie arranged herself comfortably on the bottom step and smoothed her skirt over her thighs. "I decided that she didn't kill Floraine at all."

"Indeed?" Isobel said ominously. "Who killed her?"

"Nobody," Gracie said with a bright look.

"Indeed?"

"Don't keep saying, indeed. It's so silly. All you have to do is think about it and it all comes clear. Floraine wasn't murdered at all. She committed suicide because she was crazy."

"She was crazy," Isobel said. "Go on. Miss Rudd is perfectly sane, of course."

"No, I wouldn't say that," Gracie said cautiously. "But she's not as crazy as Floraine was. You see, I got to thinking about my aunt again. Then I thought about my uncle, my aunt's husband. And anyway, it turned out that *he* was crazy just from being around her. So I think that's what happened to Floraine. She felt herself slipping and decided to end it all."

Gracie got up and brushed off her skirt. "Do you think we ought to go and tell the others now? They'll feel better."

"I don't think they will," Isobel said sadly. "I think they'll feel much, much worse. You keep it to yourself, Gracie."

"Sure, if you really think I ought to."

"You ought to," Isobel said.

"I'm certainly glad I figured it out. We can let Miss Rudd do as she likes. Imagine—for a minute there I was scared of her, seeing that foot sticking out of the snow. Boy, was I nuts!"

"Boy," Isobel said, "are you nuts."

She turned away and began walking, not too steadily, towards the sitting room.

Gracie called after her. "Say, are you having lunch already?"

"No, I'm taking this food to a man. I found a man."

"That's swell," Gracie said enthusiastically. "I knew you could do it, even at your age. Which one is it?"

Chapter 12

WHEN SHE RETURNED TO THE SITTING ROOM Isobel found Dubois sitting where she'd left him, but there was a studied casualness in the way he sat that made Isobel believe he had been up and around examining the house. Under the circumstances he was far too self-assured, cross-country skier or not.

He had taken off his hat and Isobel saw that his hair was clipped very short and was black and curly.

He rubbed the stubble on his chin and smiled at Isobel. "You are welcome, Miss Seton."

"I'm sorry there's not much variety here, but I can't cook."

"Can't you?" he said, still smiling, but his eyes were watchful.

She put the dishes on the floor beside him and said, "You remind me of someone."

He waved a piece of bread gaily. "I am constantly reminding someone of someone. I fear I am a type. Perhaps that is why Mr. Crawford dislikes me."

"Mr. Crawford doesn't need an excuse to dislike anyone," Isobel said. "He has a creative impulse for trouble."

He continued to eat, hungrily, but delicately, picking the crumbs from his lap and tossing them into the fire. From one corner of the room a radiator began to clatter and bang. Dubois' hand poised rigidly in mid-air for a moment, then went on with the crumb-gathering.

It made Isobel nervous and she started to fidget. He stopped immediately and looked up at her.

"I see you have been under a strain," he said with sympathy.

"Yes."

"You are from the city?"

"New York."

"You have come a long way, not in actual miles, but in other things. French Canada is no doubt strange to you?"

"If what's happened to me is a sample," Isobel said grimly, "French Canada is a very strange country."

"Your experiences have been unusual?"

"Terrific is the word."

"Oh?" He nodded wisely, waiting for her to continue.

"I get on a bus and the bus-driver walks off into a blizzard. Exit permanent. I get out of the bus and am shot at. I go into a house and find an insane woman and a sinister nurse. Exit the nurse. Very permanent."

"Ah yes, the body. Mr. Crawford took it into the other room?"

"The library," Isobel said. She frowned suddenly, and thought, why the library? He knew I wanted to go in there. Is he trying to keep me out?

Dubois said, "You distrust Mr. Crawford?"

"I don't feel one way or the other about him," Isobel said. "I have no reason to trust any of these people. I have never seen them before, except a picture of Mr. Goodwin in a newspaper once."

Picture in a newspaper. There was something queer about the phrase which gnawed at her mind. There was something about a picture in a newspaper . . .

Dubois was talking again and she turned her attention back to him.

". . . any reason to suspect that the nurse was murdered? May it not have been an accident of some kind?"

"I don't know. There were no marks on her. She apparently fell or was pushed over the second-story balcony."

Dubois leaned forward. "But surely a fall in soft snow wouldn't kill her?"

"The balcony's very high. See how high the ceilings are in the house."

"But even so . . ."

"And perhaps she had heart trouble," Isobel said, "and died of shock as she fell."

"That is possible. This balcony runs along the house?"

"Yes."

"Both sides?"

"Yes."

"Which side did she fall from?"

Isobel pointed. "Outside the library. It happened during the night. Paula Lashley heard her scream."

"I must become acquainted with these people," Dubois said. "Who was occupying the room directly above the library?"

"She was, Floraine herself."

"And the next room?"

"Miss Rudd."

"I am full of questions," he said, smiling. "I am interested in mysteries. So profound a one as this makes me forget I am a guest here and have no right to ask questions."

"You're not my guest," Isobel said dryly. "Ask away."

"It seems odd," he said, "that Miss Rudd who lived amicably alone here with her nurse should decide to kill her. You agree?"

"Yes."

"I hope I may see Miss Rudd. One can estimate many things about a person from his or her appearance. Character is written on the face. I find Mr. Crawford, despite his unfortunate manners, an eminently honest man who is still emotionally immature. He could be persuaded, I fancy, to play cops and robbers. He is still a boy."

"Well, he has some very boyish habits," Isobel said wryly. "And I don't believe you can read character from faces. You don't look like a cross-country skier, for instance."

"Perhaps you've never met any."

"I've met athletes. They don't look or talk like you."

He laughed. "Perhaps I looked and talked like this before I became an athlete. Your filing-system is too simple, Miss Seton. You have no file marked 'miscellaneous'."

"I'll whip one up," Isobel said, "and you may be the first one to get into it."

"Thank you. Who has been taking charge of the group since you arrived?"

"Taking charge?"

"Yes. There is always someone within a group who decides what the others will do or eat or wear or talk about."

"Not in this group. I've tried. I wasn't a success, thanks to Mr. Crawford's heckling and the natural laziness and selfishness of most of the others. The difficulty is that none of them has any sense of responsibility. A woman is killed—but it's nobody important. A bus-driver disappears, we are shot at—but the driver doesn't matter to them personally and no one was hurt from the shooting. You see?"

"I see."

"I didn't mean to tell you all this, but since you are here you might as well know what you're in for."

"I shall not be here long."

"That's what *we* thought," Isobel said. "But here we are. Would you like some more tea?"

"Yes, thank you," Dubois said.

Isobel found Crawford in the kitchen alone. He was standing on a chair peering into the top cupboards, making groaning noises.

"What are you looking for?" Isobel said crossly. "Or shall I guess?"

"You guess," Crawford said.

"Miss Rudd?"

"Nope."

"Weevil-killer?"

"Getting close."

"Crawford Special?"

"You have it," Crawford said. "I am looking for some of that nice fiery liquid that makes Crawford feel he is a king among men."

"I thought Crawford always felt that way," Isobel said. "It's Crawford's acquaintances that have to be convinced. Move over. I want the teapot."

Crawford stepped down from the chair and watched her pour out the tea.

"Is that for our skiing champ Dubois?"

"Yes."

"Nice-looking fellow, Dubois, but he hasn't my rugged charm. Of course that's only *my* opinion."

"You said it," Isobel replied coldly. She started to walk away, then turned around again and faced him, frowning. "Mr. Crawford, I want to talk seriously to you."

Crawford leered at her. "Ha, I knew you'd come around to my way of thinking about me."

"Did you take away the bus-driver's coat from the closet?"

"Yup."

"What for?"

"I wanted to examine it in the privacy of my bedroom."

"I don't believe it. As far as I can see you're trying to prevent anyone from finding out anything about anything."

"Fine, flowery English," Crawford said. "And don't breathe on the champ's tea, Isobel, you'll freeze it."

"You are deliberately, wilfully, hindering investigation to protect yourself. You don't want me to find out anything about you . . ."

"You go carp at the champ, Isobel. I'm busy."

"Stop calling him the champ! He's a very nice, polite, sympathetic and intelligent man. . . ."

"You'll get over this infatuation, Isobel, and then you'll come back to me. He is dross and chaff, flotsam and jetsam, a homewrecker . . ."

The door slammed. Crawford gazed at it, grinning. Then he started to whistle and climbed back on the chair and resumed his search for another bottle of brandy. He didn't find any brandy but he found a pint of Seagram's rye. With the bottle in his pocket he went upstairs very quietly, and into Isobel's room. He caught sight of his face in the mirror above the fireplace. It was stiff and triumphant, and he smiled at himself. He was in a tight spot and it excited him, made him reckless.

He moved quickly around the room, with the smile still plastered on his face and the blood racing through his veins.

In three minutes he had found what he wanted, and five minutes after that it was destroyed.

He stood watching the flames leap up the chimney and his triumph bubbled up in his throat. It wasn't the triumph of winning because he hadn't won, and there was a good chance that he wouldn't win—but he liked the challenge, he liked to out-talk and out-think other people, he liked to fight, even when the breaks were all against him as they were now. From the time he had tried to start the bus and failed, his luck had been out.

But he always bounced back somehow. Even Floraine's death, after the first shock was over, had exhilarated him in some strange perverse way—he knew now he had a mortal enemy in this house, someone who knew him and what he was and someone he didn't know.

A mortal enemy. Someone who wore a mask like himself, but not so subtly as he wore his. You had to be subtle to carry things off as he did, telling the truth in such a way that you weren't believed. He was good at that. He had fooled Isobel Seton.

Or have I? he thought in a moment of self-doubt. Have I fooled her? Or has she fooled me? I'd better watch my step.

It would be funny if it were Isobel. Funny and damned exciting and dangerous.

He went back into the hall and stood for a minute, listening. The others were all downstairs. He could search their rooms now if he wanted to, but he knew it wouldn't be any use. He was up against someone too clever to leave behind any evidence that would crack the mask.

I'll have to think, *think,* he said silently, but there was this queer excitement in his head that prevented him from thinking, and he had had too much brandy.

I'll go down and tell them all that I've moved the body, he thought, I'll get them circulating around again and watch. Perhaps I'll get them looking for Frances and give them something to do. It will be safer for me not to have them all together.

At the thought of Miss Rudd he frowned suddenly and some of the excitement left him. He had been afraid of her. She had been after him with that chair . . . yes, she'd better be found. And he didn't want to be the one to find her.

Upon reaching the dining room he discovered that the rest of the group shared his feeling very strongly.

"I think it would be far, far better," said Mrs. Vista, "if we all remain in one room and leave Miss Rudd the rest of the house. Don't you think so, Anthony?"

Mr. Goodwin thought so, yes.

Mr. Hunter coughed gently and said, "I shouldn't mind looking for Miss Rudd, but I shouldn't like to find her."

"Oh, Poppa," Joyce said petulantly. "You're always trying to spoil things for me. I think Mr. Crawford is perfectly right. But if we're going to look for her we shouldn't go alone, but in *pairs.*" She looked across at Chad Ross and gave him a dazzling smile. "What do you think, Mr. Ross?"

Chad Ross, receiving a long cold stare from Paula which followed the dazzling smile, said, "No. I mean yes."

Paula raised her brows. "Just what do you mean?"

Joyce smiled sweetly at her. "He means he's agreeing with me."

"Don't fight over him, ladies," Crawford said dryly. "I don't think he can handle both of you."

Chad looked at him. "You can, I bet."

"I'd die trying."

"Are you being coarse?" Mrs. Vista said, gazing at him sternly. "I don't approve of coarseness, especially in the dining room, in front of minors. Anthony's poems are sometimes brutally realistic, but never, never coarse, are they, Anthony?"

Mr. Goodwin said no, never.

"Who *cares* about his poems?" Maudie said irritably.

Mrs. Vista and Mr. Goodwin exchanged sad and knowing glances.

"A philistine," said Mrs. Vista.

"Quite," said Mr. Goodwin.

"Hoi polloi."

"Definitely."

"An ignoramus."

"The very word."

"Are you talking about me?" Maudie demanded. "You triple-chinned, fat-headed old drizzle-puss?"

"Now, Maudie," Herbert said. "Now, angel."

"Oh, for God's sake," Crawford said. "I thought we were talking about Miss Rudd."

"You frog-faced, bat-eyed stinkaroo," said Maudie.

"The instant I laid eyes on that woman," Mrs. Vista said regally, "I knew her for what she was. She is *coarse.*"

"Now, now Maudie," Herbert said. "Remember your heart. Remember your blood-pressure."

"Remember Miss Rudd?" Crawford said.

"Remember Pearl Harbor," Gracie said brightly. "I think this is a cute game."

"Shut up!" Crawford roared. "Everybody shut up except me!"

Crawford's voice being what it was, everybody shut up more from shock than a willingness to oblige.

Crawford continued, more quietly, "Personally I don't care whether Miss Rudd slits all your throats. The only throat I'm anxious to protect is my own because the Crawford tenor is famous in bathrooms from coast to coast. So if nobody else wants to find her, I do and I will. And when I find her I'll give her my gun to play with, run like hell into my room, lock the door and let her shoot up the works. How do you like that for a cute game?"

There was a silence. Then Mrs. Vista said thoughtfully, "It sounds rather—strenuous. I think perhaps, with certain exceptions, we should all help Mr. Crawford to look for Miss Rudd. One of the exceptions will, naturally, be myself. I no longer possess the necessary *élan* for such pursuits, to say nothing of the necessary *joie de vivre* and *feu de joie.*"

Mr. Goodwin blinked and said he too lacked these three necessary qualities; but after being hauled to his feet by Crawford he admitted he might work them up. Since Mr. Goodwin's case was settled, he wandered out into the hall and stared helplessly up and down. Confronted by space free of Miss Rudd, he took heart and ventured to open a door which looked promising. It happened to be the library door—Mr. Goodwin was not fortunate in these matters—and he closed it again very quickly. Floraine was not a sight calculated to cheer the heart, and Mr. Goodwin retreated to the dining room looking bilious.

"Back again?" Crawford said grimly.

"My dear Anthony!" Mrs. Vista exclaimed. "Your face is positively mildewed. Really, we cannot take chances with your health. Poets are so delicate. You must remain here with me."

"I want to go with Chad," Joyce said.

"You shall go with *me*," Mr. Hunter said.

"No, Poppa, you're so dull."

"I have never been considered dull."

"People were just too polite to say so, Poppa."

"Shut up!" Crawford roared again. "And get out! All of you! Get—out—of—my—sight! SCRAM!"

There was a general movement towards the hall. In less than a minute Mrs. Vista found herself alone with Maudie.

Mrs. Vista sniffed audibly and turned her eyes to the ceiling.

Maudie drew in her breath.

"You addle-pated, bulbous-nosed old bat."

"Coarse," Mrs. Vista said sadly, with her eyes turned upwards. "A very coarse little bitch."

Chapter 13

DUBOIS SURPRISED AND DISPLEASED ISOBEL BY quite suddenly going to sleep in the middle of one of her sentences. He lay with his head propped against the back of the chair, but even in sleep his body seemed to have a watchful rigidity.

She waited, hoping the banging of the radiators or the shuffle of feet and the sound of raised voices from the hall might waken him again. She felt lonely without him. His self-assurance calmed her.

Finally she rose and went out into the hall and found Mr. Goodwin. The others had disappeared, either up or down, and Mr. Goodwin, for lack of anything better to do, was trying to play a tune on the crystal chandelier by tapping it with his cigarette holder.

When he saw Isobel he dropped the cigarette holder and looked sheepish.

"Yes?" Isobel said curtly. "What are you supposed to be doing?"

"Precisely my question," Mr. Goodwin said. "What am I supposed to be doing? Nobody told me."

"Well, think of what the rest are doing and do that. Where are they all?"

Mr. Goodwin shrugged. "Here and there. Looking for Miss Rudd. Waste of time."

"Why a waste of time?"

"It's her house. Probably she knows plenty of nooks and crannies where she can hide, supposing hiding is desirable, as no doubt it is."

"This isn't a nook-and-cranny house," Isobel said. "She's probably just in a closet upstairs."

But when Crawford and Joyce and Chad and Mr. Hunter came down they were willing to swear that Miss Rudd was not upstairs. Every available space had been searched, including the bathroom and the back staircase, and Miss Rudd had not appeared.

"It's damn funny," Chad said. "If she was a normal person I'd say she was tricking us some way, making monkeys out of us. But—this is the third one."

"Third one?" Joyce echoed.

"Third one to disappear," Chad said slowly.

Joyce's eyes widened. "She wouldn't be out in the snow?"

"No," Crawford said. "I looked out of all the windows and there were no marks on the balcony and no marks below, and it hasn't snowed since she disappeared."

"The third floor," Isobel said. "Perhaps that door really does open and it fooled us."

Both Crawford and Mr. Hunter disagreed with her.

"Maybe Paula and Herbert and Gracie have found her down in the cellar," Joyce said.

But when Paula and Herbert and Gracie came back Miss Rudd was not with them.

"This is *insane*," Isobel said shrilly. "She must be somewhere. I'm going to look myself."

"Go ahead," Crawford said. "If you think you're so much better at it."

"Will anyone come with me?" Isobel said. "Mr. Goodwin?"

"Me?" Mr. Goodwin said.

"Comic relief only," Isobel said coldly. "I need some to steady my nerves."

"Oh, quite. Know just how it is. You find me amusing?"

"You'll never know," Isobel said and walked off down the

hall with Mr. Goodwin trailing behind her. The others watched in grim silence.

How often have I been down in this cellar now, Isobel thought, pausing at the top of the stairs. I practically live here. But I can't get used to the smell.

Mr. Goodwin noticed it too. "Lime," he said. "Like a morgue."

"And rotting potatoes."

"The macabre note, yes," Mr. Goodwin said, advancing carefully into the main room.

"I've already searched this room," Isobel said. "There's no place for anyone to hide."

"The trunks?"

"I've looked there before," Isobel said, barely glancing at them.

Mr. Goodwin went and looked at the trunks. "I haven't seen a trunk like this for years. Reminds me of when I was a boy . . ."

"Were you ever a boy?" Isobel called from the next room.

There was a long and noticeable silence after this, no sound at all from Mr. Goodwin.

Now what? Isobel thought and came back into the main room.

The lid of the trunk was open and Mr. Goodwin was crouching beside it, like a tiger motionless before its prey. But his face was dreamy.

"She is here," he said in a deep strange voice.

Miss Rudd seemed small in death, and helpless. The wild look had gone from her face and she was only a little old woman curled up in a trunk to sleep for a time. Her eyes were closed and her hands were clasped under her chin, and her tongue stuck out of her mouth in a roguish way.

"She was a child," Goodwin said, "a child who lived too long."

It was a gentle epitaph. Isobel began to cry almost without sound.

"Hush," he said. "This is hardly death. She is warm and soft and happy."

"No, no, don't talk like that. She was killed—*killed!*"

"Yes. The bruises on her neck," he said, but he still looked dreamy. "She is not like the other one. She died easily, perhaps gladly."

"Someone closed her eyes afterward," Isobel whispered. She looked again at Miss Rudd and for a moment she saw her as Mr. Goodwin saw her, as a child who should have died before and was glad to die now. But she said again, "No, no! Someone killed her! I can't see it as you do."

Mr. Goodwin straightened and closed the lid of the trunk, and once the lid was closed he seemed to change back to what he had been. The change was so sudden and so intense that Isobel thought, that's the first glimpse I've ever had of him, the first sight backstage behind the curtains.

"Frightful," he said in his old voice and walked upstairs ahead of her, muttering to himself.

Crawford was waiting in the kitchen and when he saw Isobel's face he didn't have to be told that Miss Rudd had been found.

He said, "Dead?"

"Yes," Isobel said.

"How?"

"Strangled."

"With a rope?"

"No," Isobel said huskily. "With fingers."

"How long ago?"

"I don't know. I didn't touch her."

"She was still warm," Mr. Goodwin said. He went away, looking impatient because death had interfered and made him step out of character.

Crawford looked down at Isobel. "You know what this means?"

"Yes."

"One of us killed her. One of us killed Floraine."

"Yes." She stirred under his steady gaze.

"I think now you were right," he said. "We must try and get help. One of us will have to try it."

"Mr. Dubois . . ."

"Can we trust Dubois?" Crawford said.

"I don't know. I think so."

"I don't. He might go off and not come back and not send anyone for us. How do we know he came here by accident?"

"Someone could go with him," Isobel said. "There are the snowshoes and Dubois could ski slowly, perhaps. We'll *have* to trust him. And even if—if we can't—you have a gun."

"A gun?"

"You could take the snowshoes. If you had the gun he wouldn't try to leave you behind. You could shoot at him."

He said, "Well," with a grim little smile.

Isobel flushed and said, "I meant, as a last resort. What

do you carry a gun for if you look so shocked when someone suggests using it?"

"Not shocked. Surprised. At you."

"I don't care. Something has to be done."

"I've never been on snowshoes," he said.

"Yes, but it's a bright day and not noon yet. And surely Dubois will know something about directions if he's really a skier."

"If."

"And there's no one else who can go with him. You know that."

"I'll talk to him," Crawford said. "If he refuses to talk shall I shoot him?"

"Don't joke about it."

"I'm not," he said dryly.

When he had gone she stood for a minute staring blindly at the floor. Then she turned and walked slowly into the dining room.

Mr. Goodwin had said nothing about finding Miss Rudd, for the others were still speculating on where she could be.

He's a coward, Isobel thought, he's left it to me. And I won't tell them, I *won't* . . .

But then Joyce looked up with a malicious little smile and said, "Well. Where's the loot?" And Isobel found herself saying, "In the cellar. She was in the cellar."

"But we looked all over the cellar," Paula said, frowning.

"Not in the trunks."

"Trunks?" Gracie repeated. "But you told me before they were empty!"

"They were," Isobel said, "before."

"You mean she's dead?"

"Yes."

"I told you," Gracie said hoarsely into the silence that followed. "I told you she wouldn't hurt anything. She was a harmless old lady. She never hurt anything."

Gracie began to weep quietly. Everyone else seemed incapable of moving or talking.

"I knew," Gracie said, her voice muffled with a handkerchief. "I knew it wasn't her that killed the cat. She wouldn't have put it on my bed. She liked me. She—she even gave me a present."

"Who killed it then?" Isobel said quietly.

"Floraine. She did it. She wanted to make sure we went away. She wanted to get rid of us by scaring us."

I believe her, Isobel thought. I believe Floraine killed the cat.

Why was she so anxious to get rid of us? Was she afraid we'd find the bus-driver? Was she afraid of one of us? Was she expecting someone to come here that she didn't want us to see?

Of course. Dubois.

She was waiting for Dubois. And when he came Floraine was dead.

And who had killed her?

Isobel looked around at them, one after another, Gracie crying behind her handkerchief, Maudie twisting her thin hands, Mrs. Vista whispering to Mr. Goodwin, Herbert and Mr. Hunter grave and pompous in the face of death but utterly unmoved, Chad Ross, in a corner with Paula and Joyce, far too unhappy at his own plight to think about Miss Rudd.

Gracie was talking again. "I knew Floraine killed the cat because she shot at us, trying to keep us away."

"Funny," Isobel said, frowning. "Why didn't she keep on shooting?"

"She didn't want to *kill* anyone, just to scare us off."

"Or gain time," Isobel said. "She delayed us fifteen minutes at least that way, long enough to get rid of the bus-driver."

"Oh, stop this gruesome talk," Maudie cried. "I can't bear it."

"If you want to go up to your room," Isobel said clearly, "there's nothing to stop you now. Miss Rudd is dead."

"When one looks at it in an impersonal light," said Mrs. Vista, "Miss Rudd's death improves the situation. We can now move freely about the house, confident that no one will spring at us."

"Can we?" Isobel said.

"What a pessimist you are!" Mrs. Vista said acidly. "Who else is there to spring at one?"

"With Floraine and Miss Rudd both dead, it leaves things among ourselves, doesn't it?"

Mrs. Vista frowned and turned to Mr. Goodwin. "She's an uncomfortable woman, Anthony. I feel it best to ignore her in word, thought and deed."

"Oh, yes, yes, quite," said Mr. Goodwin.

At any other time Isobel might have laughed at Mrs. Vista but the woman's attitude, more than her words, whipped up Isobel's rage. She faced her.

"Has it ever occurred to you that *you* are as likely a suspect as the rest of us, *you* could have killed both of them?"

"Oh, nonsense," Mrs. Vista said feebly, but she moved uneasily under Isobel's stare.

"And that goes for all of us," Isobel added. "Mr. Crawford is trying to arrange to go and get help for us. We can't stay here together another night."

"Well, who on earth wants to?" Paula said.

"You do," Joyce said sweetly.

"Oh, dry up," Chad said, "both of you."

He turned to Isobel. "Why Crawford? And how's he going to get help?"

Isobel explained, but before she had finished Crawford himself appeared and said that his arrangements with Dubois were completed. They would leave directly after lunch, as Dubois said he wasn't able to leave immediately.

Isobel went over to Crawford and whispered, "How did he take it?"

"All right. Seemed anxious to oblige, in fact. He's asleep again."

"How do you feel?"

"I feel swell," Crawford said dryly. "There's nothing like the prospect of being frozen to death to cheer you up. How would the ladies like to rustle up a little food for the hero?"

"What hero?" Chad said.

"Me, Redhead. And if I didn't want to conserve my energy . . ."

"Sure, sure. You're tough."

"Maybe I don't need to conserve my energy," Crawford said slowly. "Come over here and let's find out."

Isobel deftly stepped into Chad's path. She said severely, "Don't look for trouble, Mr. Ross. No more personal feuds. We want to get out of this place some time today."

Spurred on by the hope of rescue, most of the ladies moved into the kitchen. Paula stayed in her corner, looking white and angry. When Chad came over to her she flung off his hand from her arm.

"Don't be loathsome," she said. "And childish. And stupid."

Chad smiled wryly. "It's a tall order, but I'll try. Why so glum? I thought you'd be very glad to get out of here and back to mamma."

"I shall."

"Cheer up. I won't track you down. This time."

"That's obvious. You're already making a fool of yourself over that girl."

"Why not?" Chad said. "Do you think I'm going to sit around until Mamma Lashley decides I'm worthy? Of course technically we're married, and I could be damned unpleasant over a divorce."

"There won't have to be a divorce," Paula said. "We haven't—that is, we haven't . . ."

"No, we haven't, have we? Lack of opportunity? Or lack of female hormones?"

"Don't be vulgar."

"Yes, it's a vulgar subject. Mamma taught you all about it, sure. All Men Are Beasts, that sort of thing. And besides, think what you'd be giving up if you stayed with me. What's your allowance, two hundred a month? Well, in three weeks I'll be in the army and my allowance will be about one-quarter of that."

Paula turned her face away.

"So looking at it from every angle," Chad continued, "you're a wise, wise girl. I'm the dumb bunny. I looked at it from just one angle—I loved you and I was going away."

"I can't stand it," Paula said in a low voice.

"What can't you stand?"

"Your going away."

"Oh, for God's sake," Chad said, in exasperation. "You can't stand me and you can't stand my going away. Make up your mind. Just give me a clue. That's all I ask, one single clue to the maze that passes for your mind."

Paula held her head high. "You needn't insult my mind. There's nothing the matter with my mind, but I can't help thinking of alternatives. I mean, I'm like Hamlet."

"So you're like Hamlet. I'm glad you put it like that. It clears the air nicely. All is now explained. All right, go ahead with the divorce, annulment, or whatever you want. I've had the shortest marriage in history, anyway, and that's something."

Paula looked at him, tearful and angry.

"You aren't being fair to me. I didn't want to run off like this and get married. I wanted to make mother see . . ."

"You tried that before. Twice. Don't you ever catch on? She doesn't object to *me* personally. It's all men, all the men who might take her little Paula away from her. No, Paula. You're stuck. You're glued to her for the rest of your life. You're the virgin sacrifice on Mamma's altar."

"Why, you're mad! Mother is one of the most charming, civilized, cultured people in the world!"

"What's the use of talking?" Chad said quietly. "There's only one word for your mother and you know what it is."

He went out and she could hear him going upstairs, not stamping up as he had before, but quietly as if he'd made his decision and was calm about it.

Paula remained in the chair. Her face felt stiff and her

throat ached because she wanted to cry and didn't know how. It was one of the things her mother had taught her, not to cry, to be self-controlled and poised. If you didn't lose your temper you had the upper hand . . .

Who *wants* the upper hand? Paula thought desperately. I'd rather cry and scream, I don't want to be frozen like this!

She called "Chad!" but he didn't hear her, or if he did he paid no attention.

She thought, he may be right about everything else, about me too, but not about Mother. She's the nicest person in the world. Even Father admits that.

Every year on her birthday Paula received a check and some phrase like, "Your mother is a remarkable woman." Paula remembered her father as a thin, gently ironic man.

She wondered suddenly if the remarks about her mother had been ironic. All these years he may have been throwing out hints, Paula thought. No, that's impossible. Mother *is* a remarkable woman. She's understanding, and calm and detached . . .

And cold, she thought suddenly. She's cold. She's detached because she doesn't get emotionally involved, and calm because nothing touches her. Not even me, or my happiness—or father . . .

Joyce came back into the room. "I've been crowded out of the kitchen," she said. "Where's Chad?"

"How should I know?" Paula said distantly.

"I'm willing to bet you do," Joyce said, smiling. "You're terribly transparent. I wanted to see what you'd do if I snuck up to Chad, and you burned."

"Really?"

"Positively *burned*. I'm majoring in psychology and I'm always making little experiments on the side."

"It's too bad your father doesn't make a little experiment on your backside," Paula said.

"Oh, Poppa—he's a mediocrity. He's one of these timid people, too timid to enjoy life, afraid to take a chance. Something like you."

Afraid to take a chance. Paula repeated the words silently.

"That's why I know *he* didn't commit these murders," Joyce said in a detached voice as if she were talking about a species of beetle. "I'm using psychology, of course, to find out who did."

"Oh?" Paula said.

"So far, no luck. Though as far as psychology goes, I'm the best bet in the group."

"Oh?"

"Of course. I am both passionate and controlled, ideal type for murderers who murder for good sensible reasons like money. Am I boring you?"

"Hardly," Paula said. "After all, I've never talked to an ideal murderer's type before, let alone a mere murderer."

"Well, you must have talked to a murderer," Joyce said sensibly. "But it's terribly hard to figure out who's it. If we only knew the reason why Floraine was murdered we could make some eliminations. I think there are quite a few in the group who are capable of murder but for different reasons."

"Even me?" Paula said.

"Of course. But you'd have to have an emotional reason —like protecting your child or something. But you haven't any child, so I think I'll eliminate you."

"Thank you."

"Mr. Crawford might murder someone just for fun and games. He's the exalted type, nothing fazes him. Maudie Thropple might murder for revenge. She's vindictive and not sure of herself. Both Mr. Goodwin and Gracie Morning might commit murder for money."

"Mr. Goodwin?" Paula said, smiling. "I don't think so."

"Well, look what he's going through already for money! I think tagging along behind Mrs. Vista would be harder than taking a chance on the gallows. As for Mrs. Vista, I find her in a way the most puzzling of the lot. I think she might kill someone and yet could convince herself afterwards that she hadn't done it at all. She and Mr. Crawford would be the *dangerous* types. And Chad—well, Chad takes everything out in talking and he'd probably talk someone to death."

"Indeed?" Paula said coldly. "And Miss Seton?"

"I don't believe Miss Seton would murder anyone, not at her present stage of development. Her conflict is a sexual one—she is seeking a mate. I think she has her eye on Poppa, but of course I can't allow that."

"Can't you?" Isobel said from the doorway. She came into the room, her eyebrows raised in Joyce's direction.

Joyce was not at all embarrassed. She said coolly, "All women of your age are unconsciously seeking mates."

"That's very nice to know," Isobel said. "I'll have to watch myself, won't I?"

"Oh, no," Joyce said. "Let yourself go, of course. But not in Poppa's direction."

"I have never looked at your father with anything but kindly and tolerant amusement."

"Well, a lot of women do start out like that and then work up. I took a course in H. L. Mencken." Joyce smiled benignly at the two women. "I hope I've cleared up a few things."

"You smug, officious child," Isobel said.

"My professors say I'm very objective for my age," Joyce said. "I can't help observing things accurately. I hope I haven't offended you."

She went out with a cheerful wave of her hand which Isobel found very exasperating.

"Imagine," she said slowly, "imagine seeking a mate when *she* goes along with him."

"Perhaps that's why she does it," Paula said with a wry smile. "She's a wise child."

"What was she talking about?"

"Murderers and murders and her own peculiar talents in that field."

"Oh." Isobel turned away, frowning. "She seems rather mature along certain lines, doesn't she? But perhaps she has to be to make up for Poppa's immaturity."

But Paula was no longer listening. Her thoughts had returned to Chad and the haunted unhappy look came back into her eyes. Perhaps the girl is right, she thought, and I'm afraid to take a chance, I'm too timid to live.

Mrs. Vista sailed into the room with a pile of plates and a virtuous look in her eye.

"Where is that snippet?" she demanded. "She was supposed to be setting this table."

"I'll do it," Paula said listlessly.

"Well, I should think so," Mrs. Vista said in a tone of indignant righteousness. "I cannot be everywhere at once, and Mr. Crawford must be fed adequately before he sets out to risk his life for us."

It was apparent that Crawford had been working on Mrs. Vista with some success. It was also apparent, later on, that as Crawford's stock went up Mr. Goodwin's went down. There was a strange speculative expression in Mrs. Vista's eye when she gazed at Mr. Goodwin across the table.

Mr. Goodwin, aware of the expression and conscious that he was slipping, chewed his beans and bread very mobilely, and let a glazed look come into his own eyes. It was Mr. Goodwin's composing look, but far from having the desired effect, it caused Mrs. Vista to wince quite audibly, and turn her attention to Crawford, the hero of the day.

Crawford was doing his best to look like a hero, and except for the occasional wink he gave to Isobel, he was succeeding.

No one paid much attention to Dubois, and this fact Isobel found strange until she studied him more closely. He seemed to have changed, he looked smaller, almost inconspicuous, and he ate quietly and without interest. Whereas before his quietness had had an effective, almost a sinister, quality, now he appeared merely an ordinary man who didn't want to talk.

Isobel was affected by the change in him. It forced her to doubt her own impressions of him or else to credit him with extraordinary acting talent.

Or perhaps he really has changed, she thought. Perhaps Crawford really scared him.

She turned her head to look at Dubois and caught his eyes on her. He was regarding her with a blank impassive gaze, as if he had never met her before or knew her so well he was bored by her.

Then he lowered his eyes again and resumed eating.

She said, "I hope you won't find it too difficult taking Mr. Crawford with you."

He shrugged, without looking up from his plate. "I am happy to help you," he said.

"Is there any danger?"

"I think not. This part of the country is sparsely populated but not desolate. I will direct myself by the sun."

Although he had replied politely enough to her questions, Isobel felt rebuffed and uncomfortable. He seemed to have drawn a curtain over his own personality and the curtain was as opaque and strong as steel.

Isobel thought, I've felt like this before—somewhere—the same impassivity.

She stopped eating suddenly and her knife clattered to the floor. *I've seen him before,* she thought. *I've seen his picture somewhere.*

Dubois leaned down to pick up the knife and when he handed it to her their eyes met again.

He put his hand over his heart suddenly and let out a small groan and began to sway in his chair.

"I'm—sick," he said in a painful whisper. "Help me—help . . ."

He lurched to his feet, his hands clutching at Isobel's

shoulders for support. His fingers dug painfully into her flesh.

". . . help me!"

He was deathly pale and there was stark fear in his eyes.

Chapter 14

IN AN INSTANT CRAWFORD WAS ON HIS FEET AND had reached out and grabbed Dubois' arm. He hurried him out of the door, with Isobel supporting Dubois' other arm. Crawford moved so quickly and quietly that the others, deep in conversation, barely noticed that Dubois was sick.

They put him on the chesterfield in the sitting room and Crawford opened the bottle of Seagram's and forced some of the rye down Dubois' throat. Dubois spluttered and groaned and tried to sit up.

"Lie down," Crawford said. "Drink this."

Isobel, frightened and puzzled, stood behind the chesterfield. "What's the matter with him?" she asked Crawford.

"How should I know? Can you get some water or something?"

Dubois was moving his mouth but not a sound came from it.

Isobel fled from the room and came back in a minute with a glass of water.

There was no one there.

She stood, frozen, only her eyes moving around the room, frantic and wild. Then her hands began to shake and the water splashed out of the glass on her arm. But she did not feel its wetness or coldness, there was no feeling in her at all except a powerful fear which weighed her feet and chilled the back of her neck like cold wind.

"Mr. Dubois," she said, and her voice came out of her mouth in a thin trickle. "Mr. Dubois, where are you?"

Turn and run, a voice screamed inside her, *turn and run, run . . .*

Isobel felt the slight movement behind her and half turned.

"Don't move," Dubois said.

She knew, without thinking, that he had been behind the door waiting for her to come back.

"So you know me," Dubois said. "I saw you recognize me suddenly at the table." Isobel felt her knees folding and a swift black curtain blowing over her eyes. She seemed to float to the floor, feather-light, and the floor was soft as a pillow. She closed her eyes gratefully.

She did not feel Dubois picking her up and carrying her out into the hall. He staggered under her weight, and cursed, and began mounting the steps. Someone came into the hall below, and Dubois stopped halfway up and saw that it was Chad Ross.

"She's fainted," he said to Chad. "I'm taking her to her room. The strain has been too much for her."

Chad stared, but said nothing, and Dubois continued on his way. Isobel did not stir.

He put her down on the bed in the first room he came to. When he saw that she was still unconscious he left her for a moment to pour out a glass of water from the water pitcher.

He poured the water and came back to her and tried to force her mouth open. She moved slightly.

"Here," he said. "Drink this up. You fainted."

Her eyes fluttered and opened a little, and he saw by the fear in them that she was fully conscious.

"Drink it up," he said. "You don't have to be frightened of me."

"No! No, I won't drink it!" She wanted to scream but her throat seemed paralyzed and she spoke in a whisper. "No! No."

"Don't be childish," he said gently. "You cannot harm me by knowing who I am, and I have no desire to harm you."

She sat up and tried suddenly to push the water away so that it would spill. But he was prepared for this and drew his hand back quickly.

His other hand came round the back of her neck and she felt her strength leaving her. The water trickled down her throat and he didn't ease the pressure until it was all gone. Then he set the glass down carefully, and with no emotion at all he put one hand over her mouth and with the other held her arms.

"You're going to sleep now," he said evenly.

He waited until her eyelids began to close and he no longer felt her muscles struggling against his hands. Then he rose from the bed and went calmly out into the hall and closed the door behind him.

When he reached the first floor he found the other women huddled together in the hall.

Paula turned to him and said huskily. "Please. Please hurry. We have to get out of here."

Dubois said, "Where's Crawford?"

"He's getting ready," Paula said. "You'll have to help us, Mr. Dubois."

"Of course," he said politely. "I am quite ready to leave when Crawford is."

"Do you feel better, Mr. Dubois?" Mrs. Vista asked.

"Oh, yes, thank you. I just felt faint for a moment," he said.

He turned away with an impatient twitch of his shoulders. He went down into the cellar and began to put on his heavy jacket, moving quickly and precisely. He did not even glance at the trunks when he passed them.

There was too much fuss about death, he thought.

He brought his skis inside through the cellar door and examined them and brushed off the snow. Then he slung his poles over his shoulder and went upstairs again. There was no use thinking about death until the very moment it struck you. . . .

Crawford was at the front door, attempting to fasten the snowshoes to his shoes. He had his overcoat on and a scarf tied around his head and he was in a savage mood.

"You are ready?" Dubois said.

"No!" Crawford barked. "Somebody get these goddam women off my neck." He glared up at Gracie. "Do you have to stand there watching me?"

Gracie took a step back and said helplessly, "I only wanted to . . ."

"Shut up!"

"You are still not learning politeness," Dubois said mildly. "But perhaps this is not the time to demand it. You are fastening the thongs improperly. Shall I assist?"

"I'll do it myself," Crawford said roughly. "Just tell these dames to beat it."

"We were just giving you a send-off," Gracie said with resentment. "You big piece of cheese."

She felt Joyce Hunter's hand on her arm.

"Don't," Joyce said in a low voice. "Don't antagonize him."

"Well, who does he think he is?"

"Hush." Joyce scowled at her. "Where's Miss Seton?"

Gracie's eyes widened and she looked around the group. "Where's Isobel Seton?" she asked loudly.

The rest looked at each other blankly. Finally Chad

glanced dryly at Dubois and said, "She's fainted, I believe? You carried her upstairs?"

"That is correct," Dubois said blandly. "She was much affected by the excitement. She will be better after a time."

Gracie stared at him. "Yeah? She's not the fainting type and she wouldn't have missed this for anything."

Dubois said, "I am sorry I have no time to convince you. You are welcome to go upstairs and find out for yourself."

"I'll do that," Gracie said. "And don't try to leave this house until I find out if she's all right!"

Crawford straightened up and glared at her. "Who in hell are you talking about? Christ, I can't move in these things! Look at me."

"They're not for walking on floors," Dubois said, and turned back to Gracie. "I am waiting for you to reassure yourself about Miss Seton. I have no time to waste. Please hurry."

With a defiant toss of her head Gracie ran up the steps. Dubois called after her, "I placed her in the first bedroom on the left."

She found Isobel lying on the bed. She was breathing quickly and her face was pale, but she appeared to be all right.

Gracie said, "Isobel, you're O.K.? Hey, Isobel?"

Isobel did not stir. That's some faint, Gracie thought uneasily, but what else could be wrong?

When she came down again Crawford was still cursing about his snowshoes and Dubois was opening the front door.

The sun streamed in, jeweled with snow. Dubois' breath came out of his mouth like smoke as he leaned over to fasten his ski straps. When he saw Gracie he said, "You are satisfied? Miss Seton is perfectly all right?"

Gracie muttered, "Y-yes."

Mrs. Vista was bustling around Crawford, making hysterical little noises. "Be sure and come back—so upset—so grateful if you would rescue us . . ."

Crawford tightened the scarf over his ears and stepped out on the veranda. "How grateful?" he said. "And in what language?"

Mrs. Vista's hysteria disappeared, as always, at the mention of money.

"You shall be paid," she said, rather stiffly, "and paid well."

Dubois was already out in the snow, flexing his knees and jabbing the ski-poles into the snow. It was hard and crusty, with a layer of soft fine snow on top.

If I were alone, he thought, I could make speed on this ... If I were alone. . . .

Crawford stumbled down the steps after him, but he didn't curse, he was hardly aware of the snowshoes any longer because he was wondering how much money Mrs. Vista would pay him.

If I were alone, he thought, I could work this both ways. I could disappear by myself and go back to Mrs. Vista later for the money when everything had blown over. She'd be fool enough to give it to me. . . .

"Hurry up there," Dubois said.

"Sure," Crawford said. He could feel the gun swinging against his thigh as he moved. Every time it bumped him he felt the excitement rising in his throat like bubbles.

This is swell, he thought, this is a wonderful feeling. I can do anything, anything, anything . . .

It was always other people who bungled things. After this he'd go on his own. He'd be alone, free. He wouldn't have to plan anything.

His eyes glittered as if they were bright with tears.

Dubois said quietly, "Not planning anything, are you?"

Crawford's teeth showed in a smile. "Not a thing. Are you?"

"I shall be watching you," Dubois said. "Your eyes give you away."

He gripped his poles and skied off across the snow. Crawford began to walk.

"Good luck!" Paula called from the veranda. "Good luck!"

Crawford waved, and turned, following in Dubois' tracks. He moved slowly at first and Dubois was forced to lean on his poles and wait for him.

"Glide!" he shouted. "Don't lift your feet far off the snow!"

Crawford moved on, faster now, in a smooth walk almost like a dance. The snowshoes kept him on top of the crusted snow.

"Get going!" he said to Dubois. "I can keep up with you! I can keep up!"

The gun swung and bumped against his thigh, and an exultant laugh pushed up from his stomach and rang out in the still clear air. *I can keep up. I can do anything, anything. Jesus, Jesus, this is swell.*

The people watching from the veranda were suddenly quiet. Crawford's laughter struck their ears and cut into their memories.

"Look at him!" Maudie shrieked suddenly. "Look at his

face! He's not going to come back! He's running away! He's not coming back"

Crawford turned and the sun caught the gleam of his teeth and the air echoed with his sharp shrill laughing.

"Come back!" Chad shouted. "Back! Come back!"

Dubois did not even turn his head and Crawford was gliding ahead again, his head thrust high as if to meet the challenge of the cold and the sun and the brilliant air he breathed.

Chad leaped off the veranda and began to plod through the snow after them, but he could barely move in it. It was as thick and soft and treacherous to the feet as quicksand. He kept shouting and waving and calling Dubois' name. Then with a faint cry he toppled into the snow and disappeared from view.

When he stood up again he brushed the snow from his eyes and mouth, and with a weary gesture of his shoulders he made his way back to the veranda.

"It's no use," he said.

For a moment there was a hushed despairing silence in the group.

"But I offered to *pay* him," Mrs. Vista said at last. "I'm sure he'll come back."

Joyce was watching the two figures move across the snow, her face expressionless.

"Of course," she said slowly. "Of course he's not coming back. You know who he is now."

"That laugh," Maudie said. "It sounded like *her*."

"Of course," Joyce said. "He's Harry Rudd. He's her brother."

"Her brother," Gracie said huskily. "Then she was right. She wasn't as crazy as you all thought she was." Her voice rose. "I knew she wasn't! Don't let him get away! He's a murderer!"

Paula said. "There's nothing we can do. We'd better go back in the house and wait."

"Wait for what?" Mrs. Vista said bitterly.

"Mr. Dubois will send someone to rescue us," Paula said. "I'm sure he will."

But no one moved from the veranda. It was as if they had to keep Crawford and Dubois in sight as long as they could, they had to preserve this contact with the outside world. They squinted against the sun and watched the two figures become smaller until they were like ants on a sheet of paper stretching to the horizon, its whiteness broken only by scattered etchings of black winter trees.

Chapter 15

CRAWFORD BEGAN TO BREATHE HEAVILY AND there was a sharp pain in his lungs when he drew in the cold air. He stopped a minute to put his hand to his heart.

Across from him Dubois instantly braked his skis. "Don't," he said. "Keep your hands where I can see them."

"Look who's talking," Crawford said. "Very suspicious, aren't you?"

"That is correct."

"Maybe you'd like me to keep my hands in the air?"

"Very much, but I shall not ask you to. You have been useful, Rudd. I hope you have sufficient sense to keep on being useful. Shall we start again?" He did not move until Rudd did, and this time he shortened the distance between them so that they went along side by side about two yards apart.

Rudd was tiring, he could see that. He'd have to be allowed to rest frequently. If they both had skis they could be at Chapelle in two hours. As it was they'd have to take a chance and make for Gauthier's farm. Gauthier was a fervent member of the French Canada for Frenchmen organization and he'd better be willing to prove his fervency. Perhaps they could both stay at Gauthier's for a time, or perhaps Rudd had better be left there alone.

"Where are we heading?" Rudd said, as if aware of Dubois' thoughts.

"Marcel Gauthier's," Dubois said.

"All right." Funny, Rudd thought, I never even asked that before. I'm so used to his planning, so used to trusting him. But from now on, that's out. I'm me, and to hell with him.

His legs were beginning to ache from exertion. He hadn't been on snowshoes since he was twenty—probably these same snowshoes, he thought—and the sight of Dubois skimming lightly over the snow on skis filled him with resentment.

He paused again, panting, and just as he had before, Dubois stopped on a dime and looked across at him.

134

"Tired?" he said.

"Sure. What in hell do you expect?" Rudd said. "How about trading for a while?"

"That is suitable to me if you give me your gun," Dubois said. "A disadvantage must be balanced by an advantage."

Crawford patted his pocket and laughed. "The gun stays by me."

"As you say."

"I've got you, haven't I? You can't make time with me, but try going without me . . ."

"You are too emotional," Dubois said flatly. "Come along. Someone may have found the bus by this time, even though I left it on a side road."

"I suppose you're still blaming me for not being able to start it," Rudd said. "The engine was screwy."

"Excuses are nothing to me. I meet them every day."

"You bungled worse than I did!"

"I was unable to continue in the blizzard, and my foot was nearly frozen. And I had had nothing to eat and no rest all night."

"So you came back," Rudd jeered.

"I came back, yes, hardly expecting that you had brought guests with you."

"I told you. It was inevitable. I couldn't help it. If you'd let me drive the bus in the first place none of this would have happened. You could have gotten out of the bus, picked up the skis and supplies from Floraine and continued on your way north. And I could have driven right on to the Chateau. The police didn't want me then. I was safe. I would have been just another one of the guests."

"I did not trust your driving," Dubois said. "Events proved me correct, did they not?"

"The whole scheme was screwy in the first place."

"There was no time for other arrangements," Dubois said harshly. "And there is no time for talking now. You do not seem to realize the danger."

"Danger, hell!" Rudd said with a laugh.

"You will be wanted for murder," Dubois said quietly.

"They'll never catch me. I'll get out of the country. I had to kill that bitch. She was giving me away. She was calling me Harry, and she'd found the newspapers Floraine had saved."

"What newspapers?"

"The ones with your picture in," Rudd said. "Isn't that cute? Floraine saved them. Maybe she wanted to look at your pan now and then for inspiration. My hero Jeanneret!

The little French Fuehrer! Maybe I should have kept the papers for a laugh instead of burning them in Isobel's room."

"Shut up," Dubois said, "and come along."

They moved on, more slowly now. Rudd felt the excitement, the exultation in danger, leaving him. It was as if he were bleeding somewhere inside him, and the blood kept pouring out of his head leaving it blank and fuzzy.

He jerked his head back and forth to keep the blood there, to whip himself up. Then he shaded his eyes with his hand and looked around him. To the left he saw the smoke rising from a lumber camp miles away.

He grinned and thought of himself as Mr. Aldington, lumber man. I was a good Mr. Aldington, he thought. I like that name. I'll have to use it again. I'll bet that guy Hearst was surprised. I gave him a hell of a dose, maybe he's not awake yet.

He found he could get along faster if he kept thinking of things, dangerous exciting things that made the laughter form inside him.

Frances, now. It was funny how that had happened. Isobel had told him to go down into the cellar and fix the furnace. And he had, and there was Frances, hiding behind the furnace. She had said, "Harry, you thief, you murderer!" and she'd come out with a poker in her hand. So he killed her. He hardly felt the strain on his muscles, she stopped breathing so easily. But it was funny, because Isobel and Jeanneret had both been down in the cellar and hadn't noticed her there.

It was easy to put her in the trunk. She was light and small. But when she was all curled up in there he didn't like the way her eyes stuck out like marbles. He forced the lids down over them.

If they ever find out I'm Harry Rudd, he thought, that will be their clue. I closed her eyes. Because she was my sister. Like hell that was my reason.

He should have killed her long ago. She was a nuisance. He had to pay good money to have her taken care of—her money, sure, but it didn't do her any good to have money. And she was crazy. Funny how it made you feel, to have a crazy sister. Sometimes when you weren't feeling good you even suspected you might be crazy too. *But don't think about that. Think of you. Think of danger. Think of blood and snow and sun.*

Too bad he had to leave the country before he could get Frances' money. But that didn't matter much, he could always get money some place, he was clever. Damn clever.

The best trick of all had been getting them to look for Frances when he knew she was dead. It gave him a perfect excuse for going away with Jeanneret—they had to go for help. It made the escape easy.

Too bad he couldn't stop laughing there at the end . . .

Dubois had stopped suddenly and was pointing his finger to the left.

"Look," he said. "Look over there, southeast. Do you see anything?"

"Smoke," Rudd said, shading his eyes.

"No. Something moving."

"Smoke moves."

"Yes. Yes, I guess it is smoke," Dubois said uneasily. "My eyes are badly affected by this sun."

"Yes, it's strong," Rudd said, and there was something in his voice that made Dubois stare at him. But there seemed nothing unusual about Rudd, he always had the crazy glitter in his eye. He'd never attempt anything on me. . . .

Smoke, Rudd thought, he thinks it's smoke.

He looked again, and the smoke was there too but there was something else, like a moving fountain of snow. A snow-plow truck, Rudd thought. It was coming at them at right angles, and if it moved fast enough they'd be cut off.

We'll be cut off, Rudd thought, but that won't matter to Jeanneret. He can ski ahead, he can ski faster than a truck can go on these roads. He wouldn't even have to follow the roads. Jeanneret was all right. He had the skis.

But I have the gun. And if I have the gun I can have the skis.

But he'd have to watch Jeanneret, wait for his chance. Jeanneret was smooth and suspicious. And strong. Strong as an ox, but bullets can kill an ox. He wasn't as strong as a bullet.

It would be pleasant to kill Jeanneret and see his blood running out of him and making red slush of the snow. Maybe it was even his duty to kill him, to still that voice which sounded like Hitler's when he was excited, the voice that swayed peasant and student alike. Little Hitler. Little traitor.

I will kill him. I will kill him because he is a traitor and because I don't like his face and because I want his skis. I have three reasons. That is enough.

He turned and saw that Jeanneret was looking at him and that Jeanneret was afraid.

"It's not smoke," Rudd said. "I think it's a truck. I think I want your skis."

Jeanneret did not speak. His hands seemed limp on the poles and his eyelids were twitching.

"I think I'll kill you," Rudd said. His hand was in his pocket and the butt of the gun was smooth and hard and satisfying.

"Don't be crazy," Jeanneret said. "Don't be crazy . . ."

"I'm not crazy. My head feels very clear. I feel very good."

"Don't . . . I paid you. I paid you. You can't turn on me. I paid you! Don't—don't . . ."

He fell forward on his knees with his arms outstretched.

"I feel swell," Rudd said. "Little Hitler, here it is."

Jeanneret toppled, almost without sound, clutching his heart with his hands. The blood spurted out between his fingers.

Rudd stood motionless, watching him. He did not even put his gun back in his pocket but held it, prepared to shoot again. The blood fascinated him. It was like melted rubies.

Jeanneret died without a groan. Rudd touched him with the tip of his snowshoe.

"French Canada for Frenchmen," he said, laughing. "Here's your part of French Canada. Six feet by two feet. That big enough for you? Sure it is. You're not as big as you thought you were. One lousy little bullet. A cinch, Jeanneret. Heil, punk."

He put the gun back in his pocket. In the southeast the moving white fountain looked bigger. He was sure now it was a truck. Maybe with a policeman in it. Maybe Hearst had wakened sooner than he expected him to.

He bent over and took off his snowshoes. There was blood on the tip where he'd touched Jeanneret.

He slipped the pole straps off Jeanneret's wrists and the blood dripped down the poles. He rolled them over and over in the snow to get the blood off. Then he took the skis off Jeanneret's feet and tossed them to the side.

He buried Jeanneret by pushing him into the snow as deep as he'd go and when he wouldn't go any deeper he stood on him, balancing himself with the poles.

They'll find him some time in the spring, Rudd thought. And by that time—hell, by that time I'll be in South America, or Florida. I think I'll be Mr. Aldington in Florida.

He pushed some more snow on Jeanneret's body and said again, "Heil, punk!"

Then, almost without hurry, he began to put the skis on. The snow-plow truck was coming closer, but he didn't look at it again until he was ready to leave. Then he thrust the poles into the snow, and with his head raised in challenge he shouted:

"Come and get me! Come and get me, you bastards!"

He slid ahead, laughing to himself. His head felt clear and there were noises inside it like the bells of danger.

Chapter 16

THE SOUND OF THE SHOT REACHED THE VERANDA like the snapping of a thin thread.

Chad said, "We'll go inside now. No sense in waiting . . ."

"What was that noise?" Mrs. Vista said.

"How should I know?" Chad said. "Come inside."

Paula looked at him levelly. "You know what it was. It was a . . ."

"Dry up," he said.

"It was what?" Mrs. Vista said irritably. "Speak up, girl."

"It was a shot," Paula said.

Mrs. Vista blinked. "A shot? A gun, you mean?"

"Probably some farmer shooting rabbits," Chad said. "Sound travels quite a distance in this air. Nothing to get excited about. Let's go inside."

Mrs. Vista gave him a glance from her shrewd little eyes, but Chad's face remained expressionless. Perhaps it was a farmer, she thought, and even if it were not it was far far better to believe it was. She took Mr. Goodwin's arm, and leaning on it heavily she followed the Thropples and Mr. Hunter back into the house.

"Go in too, Paula," Chad said flatly.

"Are you coming?"

"Later."

"Why not now?" She nodded her head in the direction of Joyce who stood at the far end of the veranda, her eyes still fixed on the horizon. "Because of *her*?"

"No," Chad said. "I thought you and Miss Morning could go up and attend to Isobel."

Paula hesitated and her face looked sulky and defiant.

"I didn't like the way she looked," Chad added.

"You're just getting rid of me."

"That's what you want, isn't it? Be reasonable just this once. Let your right hand know what your left is doing."

A slow flush spread over her face. Then, without any warning, she raised her hand and dealt him a stinging blow on the cheek.

"That's what my right hand is doing," she said in a high tearful voice.

"All right," Chad said quietly. "Now how about your left? You got that figured out too?"

She raised her left hand and then dropped it wearily and walked into the house. Her face was pale and stiff. *I've hit him. I've hit someone. I haven't any control. I'm jealous, jealous—I love him . . .*

She began to cry and whisper through her sobs. "I love him. I love him. I'm jealous of him and I love him."

"Sure you do," Gracie said from the staircase. "And so what. Are you coming?"

Sniffling and wiping her eyes, Paula followed Gracie slowly up the steps.

When the door closed behind Paula, Chad walked quickly over to Joyce.

"Can you still see them?"

"One of them," Joyce said. "Crawford had the gun, so I guess what I see is Crawford, or Rudd."

Chad scanned the horizon but could see nothing. "You have good eyesight, haven't you?"

"Of course," she replied, without turning. "Inside and out. I think Rudd is crazy. He acts like a maniac."

"What if he's killed Dubois?"

Joyce turned then and gave him a half-pitying smile. "That wouldn't make any difference to us. You don't suppose Mr. Dubois intended to send help to us, do you? You are *very* naïve."

"What in hell are you talking about?"

"Naïveté seems to be as congenital as color-blindness. I really believe I was sophisticated at two. I don't suppose Dubois is even his real name."

"Go on," Chad said grimly.

"As soon as I saw him," Joyce said in a dreamy and exasperating voice, "I recognized the pimples at the back of his neck. And of course, even aside from that, pure logic indicated that he would have to be the bus-driver."

"I suppose you were as logical at two as you were sophisticated."

"Naturally," Joyce said modestly. "I mean, Dubois' arrival

was coincidental. I don't suppose many skiers do get lost, and it seemed far too peculiar that we should lose a bus-driver and find a lost skier. You understand?"

"You make it very clear. All except one point: why didn't you tell us?"

"Why should I? I knew everyone would get all emotional and obscure the issue. And the issue was, if Dubois and Crawford were a pair of crooks and murderers, it would be better to have them *out* of the house. Simple logic, again."

"Yes," Chad said weakly.

"Because of course we were not actually uncomfortable here except for the presence of a murderer. Now that Rudd is gone we shall calmly await rescue."

"And you knew about Dubois right from the start?"

"Not actually right at the start. But certainly when he faked being sick at the table. And then it was Crawford-Rudd who hurried to take him out."

"Why?" Chad said. "Why fake it in the first place?"

"That's one point I don't quite see," Joyce said, frowning. "I think it had something to do with Miss Seton. We'll have to ask her."

But Miss Seton was in no condition to answer questions. She slept on, oblivious to the cold wet towels on her face and the urgent commands of Gracie to wake up.

"Maybe she's dying," Gracie said. "Maybe they poisoned her."

"Hush up," Paula said. "She's been doped, I think. We'll have to walk her."

"Walk her?"

"Walk her. Make her walk up and down the room to wear off the drug." Paula leaned over the bed and put her arm under one of Isobel's shoulders and raised her to a sitting position. "Gracie, take her on the other side. Now pull her up on her feet."

"I don't think this is such a good idea," Gracie said, and after a time Paula was forced to agree. Isobel sagged at every joint and though she looked slender she was tall and weighed more than her appearance suggested. They let her fall back on the bed.

"One of her eyelids moved," Gracie said. "Maybe if we flung her around a little more she'd wake up."

"Bring more wet towels," Paula said. She began to move Isobel's arms up and down, and after ten minutes of this and more cold towels Isobel's eyelids began to flicker no-ticeably.

"That's the girl!" Gracie shouted encouragingly. "That's right! Wake up!"

Isobel winced and put her hand slowly to her head. "My God," she whispered. "Who—is—doing—that—shouting?"

Then she opened her eyes and saw Gracie and remembered everything with a rush.

"Where is he?" she said. "You didn't—you didn't let him go?"

"Well, we sort of had to," Gracie explained. "He just sort of left."

Isobel tried to struggle out of the bed, but there was a curious heaviness in her legs and arms and she had to lie back again, exhausted.

"He wasn't Dubois," she whispered urgently. "He wasn't a skier. He was Jeanneret. The picture in the paper—he was Jeanneret."

"Well, my goodness," Gracie said. "What of it? You don't think my name is Morning, do you? Matter of fact it's Murphy."

"Keep quiet," Paula told her crisply. She looked down at Isobel. "You'd better not try to talk. It won't do any good. They're both gone, Dubois and Rudd."

"Rudd?" Isobel said. "Rudd?"

"Crawford."

Isobel closed her eyes again.

I am tired, tired, she thought. I mustn't think now. I will not think about him. I will not think how even talking to him was exciting—no, don't think. Don't think.

She moved her head and a slow ache spread through her whole body.

He lived in another world, she thought. He carried it around with him, inside him, and if you looked in at it you were afraid and fascinated and excited all at once.

"Where is he?" she said at last. "Where is he now?"

"They went off together," Paula said, "he and Dubois." She thought with a shock: why, she loved him, perhaps the way I love Chad. And he is a murderer . . .

She said to Gracie, "I think we'll leave her alone for a while. Could I bring you something, Isobel?"

"No," Isobel said. "No, nothing."

"I'll stay here," Gracie said.

And she did stay. She sat quietly in a chair for some time, not looking at Isobel.

"Hell," she said finally, "you'll meet some other guy some time. Don't let it throw you. You just let me know and I'll introduce you to a whole squadron of them. And

with your clothes and looks and figure and everything . . ."
Her voice faded.

Isobel opened her eyes and smiled slightly. "Thank you,"
she said. "Thanks, Gracie."

"You weren't honestly stuck on him anyway. It was just
a flash in the pan."

"A flash in the pan. A very neat description."

"Write it off as experience," Gracie said. "God knows you
need some."

"Shall we change the subject?" Isobel said with an impatient gesture of her head.

"We could, but I sort of like this one," Gracie said cheerfully, "especially now that I know you're not going off half-
cocked. I'm just crazy about romance." She gazed thoughtfully out of the window. "It's a funny thing, but I never get
much of it. There's just two kinds of guys in my life, the
kind that want to sleep with me and the kind that don't.
So I got to look out for myself."

Isobel stirred again. "And you do?"

"And I do. You want some more cheering up?"

"No, I guess I'm all cheered up," Isobel said soberly. She
drew in her breath and found she could say his name almost
as if it didn't matter to her. "Crawford—Crawford was Miss
Rudd's brother?"

Gracie nodded silently.

"And he killed her, I suppose. He killed her when I asked
him to go down and tend to the fire, and then he came up
to the kitchen and I talked to him. He was looking for
some brandy . . ."

"No damn wonder," Gracie said dryly.

". . . and he didn't turn a hair, he was so natural and
cheerful."

"I guess he was glad to get rid of her," Gracie said. "It's
kind of hard to have crazy relatives, you know, like my
aunt. And Miss Rudd kept giving him away. She kept calling
him Harry but nobody caught on except me and then it
was too late. I guess he actually was stealing from her, paintings, and furniture and things."

"Yes," Isobel said stiffly. "Yes."

"And Floraine helped him. Seems funny though, that he
kept up this house when he could have sent Frances away
to an institution."

"He kept her here because he was ashamed of her," Isobel
said, "and because, I think, this house had been used before
by people like Jeanneret, perhaps for political meetings or

perhaps for certain people to hide out in. I think Floraine
ran the house. I think she was—his mistress."

Gracie lowered her eyes and said uneasily, "Yeah, I think
she was."

"And he killed her because he—well, he might have just
been angry with her. He didn't need a better reason than
that."

But there was something that didn't quite fit in and for
a minute she couldn't remember what it was.

Then she thought, of course, it's the way he acted when
he found Floraine, and brought her into the house. He was
shocked, that's the word. After he killed Frances he acted
almost normal, he seemed happy in the excited way Frances
herself was happy when she brought the newspapers to
Gracie as a present.

She remembered him looking down at Floraine when she
was lying in the hall. He had looked savage and frightened
and his voice had been rough: "My nerves are bad and when
my nerves are bad I want action, any kind of action . . ."

He had come over and kissed her then, and his mouth
had been hard and cold.

He was afraid, Isobel thought. that's what fear does to
me, it makes me cold all over. What was he afraid of?

She remembered then when she had stood outside Miss
Rudd's door and listened to see if she was asleep. It had not
been Miss Rudd in that dark room. It had been Floraine,
talking to Crawford: "Don't lose your nerve. She can't do
a thing to spoil it . . ."

They were talking about *me,* Isobel thought, And if I
had rapped on Crawford's door then as I intended to, I
would have found out he was in there with Floraine. But
Joyce came along and interrupted. And Joyce had said
"Don't rely on Mr. Crawford."

Isobel thought, when he came over and kissed me in
the hall he was afraid of me. That's why he did it. He had
always to come and meet danger more than halfway. That's
why he paid so much attention to me—he thought *I* had
killed Floraine.

Gracie said, "There you go thinking about him again. I
can tell."

"Yes, I was."

"Just asking for trouble."

"I believe I am," Isobel said slowly. "I think I'm going
to ask for trouble."

She got off the bed and straightened her skirt. Her head

felt too light and her legs too heavy, but she found she could walk.

"Where are you going?" Gracie said.

"Just downstairs."

"Do you want me to come?"

"If you'd like to."

"I don't think I will," Gracie said. "I'm getting damn well sick of that crowd."

"You could do your hair again," Isobel said dryly, "and I have some nail polish in my purse you could have."

Gracie brightened. "That'd be swell."

The purse and nail polish were found and Gracie settled happily down in her room. Isobel went downstairs.

Except for Chad and Joyce Hunter, who were still outside, the group was gathered in the sitting room. Herbert and Mr. Hunter had built a fire in the grate on the theory that the sight of a nice hearth fire would enliven their spirits.

Unfortunately the only sight of the fire the others had was obtained by peering around Mrs. Vista's broad and unbeautiful backside. For Mrs. Vista was not one to consider the comfort of others, and having lived in England all her married life she was well acquainted with the strategy of hearth fires, which is to get there first.

She rubbed her hands together and said there was nothing like a hearth fire, and when Maudie acidly inquired, "where is it? *What* fire?" Mrs. Vista merely thought how ungracious she was. Coarse and ungracious.

She was rather annoyed to find herself being jostled from the rear and still more annoyed when she discovered that the jostler was Isobel Seton. For no matter how charming Miss Seton's exterior, Miss Seton was a trouble-maker and Mrs. Vista felt unable to cope with any extra trouble at the moment.

"I want to talk to you," Isobel said.

Mrs. Vista closed her eyes firmly and tried to pretend that Isobel was not there.

But Isobel was there and she proved it by clasping Mrs. Vista's arm, not at all gently.

"Did you hear me?" Isobel said.

"I suppose I did," Mrs. Vista said sadly.

"You had the room beside Crawford's, didn't you?"

Mrs. Vista said, yes, it was impossible to forget that because Mr. Crawford had snored off and on all night and she hadn't had a wink of sleep.

Isobel said, "You were in your room when you heard Floraine scream?"

"Yes, I don't care to think about . . ."

"And Paula was in the bathroom?"

"Yes."

Paula had overheard and come over to join them. "Why?" she said, frowning. "Why all this?"

"Did you hear Crawford snoring?"

"Yes, of course. You couldn't miss it," Paula said. "That's why I decided to wake him . . ."

Her voice died suddenly and she blinked her eyes.

"And if he was sleeping," Isobel said, "he wasn't pushing Floraine off a balcony."

"I won't listen," Mrs. Vista said. "I will not listen to anything more. I simply refuse."

Paula and Isobel looked at each other. Then Paula blinked again and said, "Very likely I was mistaken about hearing Mr. Crawford snore. I can't be sure."

"Of course you can't," Mrs. Vista cried. "Nor can I. My nerves . . . I'm a very *suggestible* type. Aren't I, Anthony?"

Mr. Goodwin said, oh, yes, yes, yes.

Mrs. Vista turned back to Isobel and said bitterly, "You cannot leave well enough alone. You are a trouble-maker, there is no other word for you!"

Isobel cried, "And you—you are a . . . !"

But what Mrs. Vista was to Isobel was not revealed, for a sudden shout rang through the house and Joyce came bursting into the door.

"A snow-plow!" she shouted. "There's a snow-plow coming!"

Mr. Hunter, who was acquainted with his daughter's little experiments in psychology, said, "Now, Joyce. You're sure? You're positive?"

"I," Joyce said, "am always sure."

She dashed out of the door again, and the rest followed her, with Mrs. Vista wobbling along in the rear.

Only Paula and Isobel remained, looking at each other quietly.

"You know you heard him," Isobel said at last.

"I didn't want to excite everyone," Paula said. "Mrs. Vista is rather silly sometimes, but in this case I think she was right. Leave it alone until we're out of this house."

Isobel shrugged and said, "All right. Shall we go and look at the snow-plow?"

"No." Paula turned her face away. "I'm not sure I want to see it. I'm not sure . . ."

Isobel went out and met Gracie plunging down the stairs trying to talk and blow on her nail polish to dry it at the same time. They went out onto the veranda and watched the snow-plow come slowly along the road and almost up to the veranda steps.

The whirl of snow stopped and two men got out of the truck. One of them was in uniform. He waved his hand and then began plodding his way through the snow towards the house. They seemed to move with inexorable slowness, like two fates.

"Ahoy!" Mrs. Vista shouted, and the man in uniform raised his arm and smiled. "Ahoy! You the Lodge people?"

Joyce stood apart from the rest of them, her dark eyes taking in their faces one by one, almost absently.

She knows, Isobel thought, watching her. She knows it wasn't Crawford. She's waiting for one of us to crack . . .

But no one did crack, not even Maudie, who, faced with the choice of fainting from excitement or powdering her nose, powdered her nose. Mrs. Vista tucked in a few stray wisps of hair. Mr. Hunter stroked his mustache thoughtfully. Gracie admired her nails. Mr. Goodwin had retreated into the vast chasm of his own mind.

And Isobel stood with her eyes fixed on the snow and for a minute she thought she saw Crawford poised against the sun, a strange glittering man who fled from hell to hell and had no peace anywhere.

She was barely conscious of the arrival of the two men on the veranda, the explanations, the questions, all shouted at once in every pitch.

"He went *that* way!" Mrs. Vista shrieked. "Hurry up and catch him!"

"There are two of them!" Maudie said shrilly.

Under this battery of noise Sergeant Mackay did not even blink. When things had quieted down he coughed and said in a dignified voice:

"Mackay, of the Royal Canadian Mounted Police. This is Mr. Hearst, who drives the Lodge bus."

There was a short silence. Then Gracie said brightly. "Gee, we're glad to see you! I'm just *crazy* about policemen!"

Chapter 17

"... AN ILL-TIMED REMARK," WROTE MRS. VISTA
to her sister, in the knotty pine writing room of the Lodge.
"It set the mood, as it were, for the subsequent events, and
Sergeant Mackay became friendly, not to say *intimate*. (I
do not *quite* trust a friendly Scot, do you?) Practically in
front of everyone I was forced to explain all about Cecil
and Anthony and why I came here in the first place. One
thinks one has nothing to hide and then it turns out that
one *has!* Too humiliating!

"While we were all answering this policeman's questions,
the young man called Hearst drove away in the truck and
came back with our lost bus.

"And so here we are! We arrived about six o'clock and
after the rigors to which I have been subjected I was delighted to find that the Chateau is quite a civilized place,
and the apparent ruggedness remains, as ruggedness should,
only apparent. Sergeant Mackay made no objections to our
coming here, so I presume the mystery, for him at least,
is adequately explained. At any rate we have no policemen
around guarding us, as frequently happens in fiction. But
perhaps even policemen have some sense and Mackay is
only too glad to be rid of such traitors and agitators as
Floraine and Jeanneret and that man Rudd.

"It was sheer ill-luck that we were so involved in the
events. I am still just a little foggy on the explanation, but
it seems that this man Jeanneret was a *very dangerous*
agitator who was interned somewhere near Montreal in a
reform school converted into an internment camp. At any
rate Rudd helped him to escape in a laundry truck, and
they managed to get as far as Briarée, which is where the
Montreal train line ends and where the snow-bus met us.

"The laundry truck broke down and there was a blizzard
coming on, and Jeanneret conceived the idea of stealing
the bus which, beside the snow-plow, was the only vehicle
which could get through the roads. Jeanneret could not go
back in the direction of Montreal where they were on the

watch for him, and besides. Sergeant Mackay believes that he was on his way to the important new mining area north of here. Something to do with the war, but that, of course, is a *secret!* How one goes about *agitating* in a mining area, I don't know. One can only say that it takes all kinds to make a world!

"There is a delightful man here, who teaches skiing. He escaped from Austria just after the Anschluss. I wonder if perhaps a little skiing might bring down my weight. . . ."

Mrs. Vista stared thoughtfully out of the window and saw two beginners at the top of a gentle slope. One of them started down and landed almost instantly, skis waving in the air. Mrs. Vista returned hastily to her letter.

". . . or perhaps I shall simply go on a diet. This will be difficult, as they have a magnificent cuisine here, and this morning I had real Quebec maple syrup—simply crawling with calories, of course, but perhaps I shouldn't worry about my weight *at all*. One is not expected to look like a girl at forty-five!

"The Austrian ski-meister is called Putzi, I don't know why. But I shall find out. . . ."

Mrs. Vista looked up at the sound of ski-boots tramping across the floor. It was Paula Lashley and she looked very pale, Mrs. Vista thought. She laid down her pen.

"Hello, my dear," she said heartily. "Are you going to write a letter?"

"No."

Paula went over to the window and glanced out. "I'm waiting for the bus to leave."

"Leave! Why we only came yesterday."

"I've changed my mind," Paula said curtly. "I haven't got time for skiing this winter."

"Is your young man going too?"

"He's not my young man. He's staying here."

Paula continued to stare out of the window, watching Mr. Hearst tinkering with the engine of the bus. She tapped her foot impatiently and she looked as if she didn't want to talk. But Mrs. Vista never allowed such considerations to interfere with her own desires.

"Of course he's your young man," she stated firmly. "I have observed the nasty way he looks at you. It is a sure sign."

"Really?"

"Really. Of course I am not an *old* woman, but I have *lived*. And one has only to look around one to interpret the signs of love. In just that way, Cecil used to look at me.

Among lesser animals too, my dear. Has one ever seen a gorilla give his mate a really *friendly* look? One has not!"

"I am not interested in gorillas," Paula said coldly, "with or without red hair."

She looked out again and saw that Mr. Hearst was still fooling with the engine of the bus. She began to fidget, pushing her hands in and out of the pockets of her jacket.

"I cannot understand anyone who is not interested in animals," Mrs. Vista said severely. "It would not surprise me to learn that you are a *vivisectionist.*"

With this cutting reply, Mrs. Vista gathered up the sheets of her letter and sailed out into the lobby. She caught a glimpse of Chad Ross hurrying towards the writing room and regretted her own departure, for she dearly loved scenes. But still there was nothing to be done about it, it would be far too crass to go back now.

Ah, well—she would find Anthony and he would read one of his poems to her—poor Anthony, what a pity he didn't look like Putzi. . . .

"So you're leaving," Chad said from the doorway.

Paula turned with a start. She pressed her lips together to keep them from trembling.

"Yes," she said.

Chad crossed the room, impatiently kicking aside a chair that was in his way.

"What," he said, "if I don't let you?"

"*Let* me!"

"You heard me." He reached out and grabbed both her wrists and held them. "Now scream, baby."

"You're hurting me. Let me go."

"Hell, that's not loud enough. Come on, louder."

He bent down and looked savagely into her face. "*Scream*, baby. Go on."

"I—I—I can't," Paula said in a strangled whisper. "My voice . . ."

"You can't, eh?" He let go of her wrists and stood back from her. He was smiling grimly. "You can't, eh? Not a sound?"

Paula opened her mouth, but even the whisper was gone now.

"This," Chad said, "is my lucky day. Get going."

She looked at him, her eyes wide, and her mouth moving soundlessly.

"Ladies who can't scream are my meat." He took her arm and half-carried her across the room. "Now listen. We're going through that lobby and you're going to be a nice quiet girl."

Paula shook her head violently.

"Yes, you are," Chad said, leering at her. "Or I'll tell them you've been hitting the bottle, or having an epileptic fit. Come on."

His hand tightened on her arm and they went across the lobby very quickly, Paula stumbling as she moved.

Behind the desk Monsieur Roche raised his beautiful eyebrows and said, "Ah, *la jeunesse!* Always in the hurry."

In his room Chad closed the door, locked it and flung the keys on the bed.

"Can't you scream yet?"

Paula shook her head.

"You'd better try. This is your last chance. Come on, try."

Paula shook her head again. Chad came over and put his hands on her shoulders.

"Paula," he said dryly, "you're not putting up much of a fight. Mamma Lashley wouldn't like that."

Paula lowered her eyes and said primly, "I don't believe in fighting."

He looked at her much as the gorilla looks at his mate when he has something on his mind.

It would have delighted Mrs. Vista had she been there. But she was not there. Having failed to find Anthony she was in the lobby passing the time with Putzi, whose name turned out to be Herman Grube.

Mr. Grube proved disappointing. He kept looking sternly first at his watch, then at the elevator door. He did not seem interested in Mrs. Vista's personal reactions to the Anschluss, and he was not, Mrs. Vista found, very amiable.

Far, far too serious, she decided. One could never imagine him swinging gaily to the strains of a Viennese waltz. Ah well, one never could *quite* trust an Austrian anyway. Look at Hitler.

She was not sorry when Mr. Grube rose, clicked his heels and marched across the lobby. To Isobel, emerging reluctantly from the elevator, he said severely:

"Your lesson. You are late. Permit me to ask you to be on time each morning. My services are valuable."

Startled by this attack, Isobel found herself explaining weakly, "I'm sorry, I was tired. I was all doped up yesterday, and the night before I shovelled a ton of coal and . . ." Conscious of the baffled look creeping into Mr. Grube's eyes, she stopped. "All right. I'm ready now."

Mr. Grube bowed and led the way across the lobby. These

American ladies, he thought gloomily, they do not seem sense-making. Isobel, in her bright orange ski-suit with the price tag swinging waggishly just over her rear, followed him outside. She had chosen the color especially, because she wanted all other skiers to see her plainly and be able to fend for themselves.

Mr. Grube, however, intimated in his subtle Central-European way that he did not like the ski-suit.

"The color," he said. "It is not correct. For contrast with the snow it requires merely a touch of brilliant color."

"So," Isobel said.

"So," said Mr. Grube sternly. "Here we halt."

He took her skis, examined them carefully, made a disapproving noise, and then showed her how to carry them.

"Now that we're alone together," Isobel said, "you can cut out the act, Mr. Schultz."

Mr. Grube stared at her.

"I beg your pardon, Madame?"

"Just skip the temperament. I know all about you. A friend of mine told me."

"Madame?" Mr. Grube said, looking baffled again. "You feel entirely well?"

"She said the nearest you've been to Austria is the World's Fair. You come from Ontario and your name is Schultz. Well, I don't mind that part, but I'd like to make our relations clear."

Mr. Grube opened his mouth and let out a feeble laugh.

"Ha, ha, ha. You are one of these who joke!"

Isobel felt her face becoming warm. "Come on, Mr. Schultz. You might as well admit it."

"I admit it!" Mr. Grube said with desperate gaiety. "The lesson. We proceed. How you joke, ha ha!"

He showed her how to fasten her skis.

"The heels must be free."

"Heels free. Yes, Mr. Schultz."

He looked at her sideways and edged away.

"The knees bent. Notice me."

"The knees bent. Yes, Mr. Schultz."

"Madame will please use my correct name, Grube," he said earnestly. "I cannot concentrate when I am made mock of."

He sounded so intense that Isobel looked across at him. His eyes were wide and completely bewildered.

She swallowed and said, "You know the girl who's going to dance at the Lodge?"

"Girl? Dance?"

"You know, dance for the guests as in a night club. She said you helped her get her job."

"Madame," Mr. Grube said simply. "I am confused. We do not hire dancers. Our entertainment is all sporting. I know no such girl."

"You must know her!" Isobel cried. "She knows you. You got her this job. Really, this has gone far enough!"

"It has," Mr. Grube said. "My name is not Schultz."

He was sweating now, and casting anguished glances back at the Lodge.

"Well," Isobel said weakly. "Well, well."

"You have had sufficient lesson?" Mr. Grube said hopefully. "You are tired? The sun is too strong for you, perhaps?"

"Yes," Isobel said. "Take these silly things off my feet. I've got business to attend to."

Mr. Grube moved with great agility. Isobel left him staring thoughtfully first at her skis which he held, and then at her back.

She went into the lobby and looked around. Joyce and Mr. Hunter were talking to the Thropples beside the desk. Joyce waved and Isobel came over to her. With unexpected friendliness, Joyce tucked her hand inside Isobel's arm.

"Had your lesson?" she asked.

"Not exactly," Isobel said. "I'm looking for Gracie. Has anyone seen her?"

"Don't be in a hurry," Joyce said, drawing her aside. "I've just been talking to Sergeant Mackay in Briarée. I rang him up as soon as the wires were fixed. He said that Crawford was shot resisting arrest and that Floraine died of *heart-failure*." She lowered her voice. "You're very lucky. I was afraid they'd catch on to you."

"What?" Isobel said blankly. "*What* did you say?"

"Oh, I'm not going to tell anyone, naturally. But I was pretty sure right from the first. Sexual conflict. The perfect motive. You fought with her over Crawford, when you found out she was Crawford's mistress. I heard you quarreling with her right after the cat was found."

"You must be crazy," Isobel said. "We were arguing about her putting the cat in the furnace! I never even knew she was Crawford's . . ."

"Sh!" Joyce said. "That's your story and it's very wise to stick to it." She gave Isobel a long narrow look. "You have strength of character, Miss Seton. I have decided to withdraw my objections to a rapprochement between Poppa and you."

Isobel gazed at her wordlessly.

"I think it would be intensely interesting to have a woman like you for a stepmother, and I do believe you can handle Poppa. I've been worried about leaving him alone when the time comes when I myself shall seek a mate. Poppa needs a firm hand. And so I give him to you."

With a gracious smile she went back to her father.

"Your key, Miss Seton?" said Monsieur Roche. "You wish the key?"

Isobel turned sharply. "No, thanks. Tell me, is Miss Morning still in her room?"

"Morning, Morning," said Monsieur Roche. "Yes. Morning. Yes. Room two-ten."

"Thank you."

She took the elevator upstairs and walked slowly along the hall. Two sentences flashed like neon before her eyes:

Miss Rudd was let out after Floraine screamed.

Gracie let her out.

She rapped on Gracie's door, and a cheerful voice sang out, "Come on in!" Then Gracie herself opened the door. "Oh, it's you. Well, come in. I'm doing my hair. What's the matter with you?"

Isobel shut the door and leaned against it. She said, "I think you killed Floraine."

Gracie's comb clattered to the floor. She leaned over to pick it up. "That's a funny thing to say," she said warily.

"I was stupid not to have known it before. You let Miss Rudd out of her room."

"Well, you knew that. I explained that. I felt sorry for . . ."

"I don't want to hear any more of your preposterous lies. Why on earth did you tell me that about the skiing teacher? Didn't you know that as soon as I found out the truth I'd begin to doubt all the rest of your stories?"

"They weren't lies," Gracie said sharply. "I'm not that dumb. Schultzie was fired since I heard from him."

"And the dancing business?"

Gracie looked uncomfortable. "Well, I guess I sort of exaggerated that. I'm a dancer, all right, but I've been on my uppers for awhile and I came up here to be—to be a sort of hostess. A glorified waitress," she added bitterly.

Isobel stared at her and thought, she's more ashamed of that than she is of having killed Floraine.

"You did kill her, didn't you?"

"Not exactly. It wasn't my fault. It was an accident."

"What are you going to do about it?"

"Nothing."

"You can't do nothing. You killed her. You're admitting it."

"Not to anyone but you," Gracie said. "And they can't do anything to me, because it was an accident. She tried to kill me first." She shrugged her shoulders fatalistically. "It was a case of her or me, so it was her. I pushed her over the balcony."

"The balcony of *her* room," Isobel said. "Why did you go there?"

Gracie came over and sat on the edge of the bed. "Listen, you never had to look out for yourself, did you?"

"You can make the excuses later."

"They aren't excuses," Gracie said simply. "I'm telling you why I went to her room. I told you before that I knew she shot off the rifle and killed the cat just to get rid of us. And I figured if she wanted to get rid of us so badly she had a good reason. And then I figured if she had a good reason she'd be willing to pay to keep it quiet."

"Blackmail," Isobel said.

"Well, if you want to fuss around with words, call it blackmail. I didn't call it anything. I needed money and I saw a chance to get it and I got to look out for myself. I knew there was something between Crawford and Floraine. You remember when she shot at us and Crawford made us all get down in the snow? But he stood up and waved his hat. He was signaling to her.

"And anyway I'd seen him before in a night club in Montreal and his name wasn't Crawford or Rudd. Somebody pointed him out as a smooth crook. He was scattering money around to beat hell, but there was something about him I didn't want a part of—he looked too dangerous.

"Well, anyway, there was Crawford carrying a gun and signaling to Floraine and I began to smell a plot. And then when Miss Rudd began to call him Harry, the rest of you thought she was crazy, but me, I wasn't so sure. I watched him carefully and I saw he was scared to death of her. Then I saw that there'd been a lot of things removed from the house, like pictures and furniture, and Miss Rudd kept accusing Harry of stealing. So that clicked. I was sure he was Harry Rudd, and that he and Floraine were playing a smelly game between them.

"The crazy part of it is, I didn't know what the game was till afterwards! I let on to Floraine that I knew and she thought I did. But I didn't figure it out until Miss Rudd brought me the papers with Jeanneret's picture in every one of them. Then the bus-driver's clothes that you found, and the ski-wax and Floraine being so anxious to kick us out added up. Jeanneret was the driver. He went to the house and Floraine fitted him out with skis, food and clothing. Then he went on his way. But that didn't work out on account of the blizzard.

"One thing sort of puzzled me until I talked to Sergeant Mackay. Why didn't *Crawford* drive the bus? Well, Mackay said Jeanneret didn't trust Crawford an inch. Crawford was always sort of wild, and I guess Jeanneret figured he'd handle everything himself as far as he could. And it turned out he was right," Gracie added grimly. "You never get anywhere trusting people. You got to look out for youself."

"You said that before," Isobel said dryly. "So you went to Floraine's room."

"I went to her room," Gracie said. "You were sleeping. You'd been up for a long time snooping . . ."

"That's why you wouldn't go with me, wasn't it? You didn't want anyone to get suspicious about you."

Gracie nodded. "You were sleeping pretty well and didn't hear me. Floraine's room was right next door so I went out by the balcony and rapped on her window. I could tell she thought it was Crawford because she came to the window all smiles, and opened it. I said I wanted to talk to her and she said we couldn't talk inside the house, she'd get a coat and come out.

"When she came out I told her I knew who Crawford was and what the two of them were doing, and without any warning she grabbed me by the throat. She was crazy about Crawford, she would have done anything for him. I guess a lot of women would."

"Yes," Isobel said.

"Well, she started to choke me. I wasn't very frightened because I'm strong. I can do a one-arm handstand. I didn't even scream."

"You pushed her off," Isobel said.

"She was going to kill me. I had to. She just screamed once, very faintly, as she was going over. I waited as long as I could out there and when I didn't hear anything more I figured—well, I figured she was dead and I better get back to my room. I came in our window just as Mrs. Vista began to shout. You were just waking up and you were too sleepy to notice that my feet were wet from the snow. Anyway, nobody caught on and if I acted funny, well, the rest of you were acting a little funny too.

"Then poor Miss Rudd began pounding on her door. It's funny how the rest of you kept thinking she killed Floraine when all the time she was locked in her room, and the windows locked too. Well, I thought it would be a good idea if the rest of you kept thinking that, and a good idea to keep Crawford confused. He was so scared of her, and I figured she could be a sort of bodyguard for me if Crawford caught on to me. And I also felt sorry for her, naturally, on account of my aunt, so I let her out."

She stubbed her cigarette. "I'm kind of sorry I did it now. I didn't want her to be murdered."

"Such delicacy of feeling," Isobel said.

"I'm very soft-hearted," Gracie said. "I'm always letting my heart run away with my head."

"But not very far."

"But I guess she's better off this way," Gracie added, more cheerfully.

"He's dead, too."

"Is he? My, things are certainly working out, especially for me. Though it's no job for a girl like me, being a waitress practically." She let out a sigh. "Well, I guess that's all."

"And you really think you can get away with it?" Isobel said.

"Well, my goodness, I didn't actually murder anybody. It was pure accident. Besides, nobody knows but you and me."

"It's my duty to tell the authorities. I'm sorry, but it's my duty."

"They won't believe you," Gracie said calmly. "That nice policeman thinks I'm cute, and I bet when they open her up they'll find she died of heart failure. I read about how they find things out like that, and how people's hearts may fail when they're falling."

Isobel said nothing.

"Anyway," Gracie added, "I think I should even get a medal. They were a nasty bunch of crooks, if you ask me."

"It's my duty to tell . . ." Isobel began again, but she knew how useless it was to go on. She went out into the corridor and walked slowly towards the elevator.

When she reached the lobby she saw that Monsieur Roche and Mr. Grube were in earnest and worried conversation. She approached the desk, and Mr. Grube looked at her with a feeble smile.

Monsieur Roche smiled too, but he seemed very pale.

Isobel said, "I want you to telephone for the police."

"The police?" Monsieur Roche said with forced gaiety. "The police. Ah, yes. May I ask—that is, may I ask, why?"

"I have information about a murder," Isobel said.

Mr. Grube and Monsieur Roche exchanged sickly smiles.

"Ha, ha," said Mr. Grube. "The joke again. Such a one you are for jokes!"

"Ha, ha, ha," said Monsieur Roche. "We are on to you! We perceive!"

"This is no joke," Isobel said sternly. "I said I have information about a murder and it is my duty to . . ."

"Ho, ho, ho!" Monsieur Roche doubled over, his hands clasping his stomach in mirth.

Every eye in the lobby had turned towards the desk and the orange ski-suit with the dangling price tag. Roars of laughter began to echo through the room.

Isobel turned and ran wildly towards the steps.

Monsieur Roche sobered instantly.

"Every year we get such a one," he said gloomily. "Me, I do not understand it."

"Also me," said Mr. Grube.

At the first bend in the steps Isobel paused to catch her breath. Through the window on the landing she saw a cutter go past with a flutter of snow and bells.

A voice behind her said, "I have quite a way with horses." Isobel turned and regarded Mr. Hunter.

"How nice for you," she said. "*And* them."

"I was wondering," Mr. Hunter said, undeterred by a certain coldness in Isobel's eye. "I was thinking perhaps you and I could go for a cutter ride."

"No doubt Joyce is behind this invitation?"

"Well, in a manner of speaking, yes. But I concur." He leaned towards her and looked almost wolfish for a moment. "I *violently* concur."

"Well," Isobel said faintly, "in that case, I don't mind if I do."

ABOUT THE AUTHOR

Margaret Millar was born in Kitchener, Ontario, Canada, and educated at the Kitchener Collegiate Institute and the University of Toronto. In 1938 she married Kenneth Millar, better known under his pen name of Ross Macdonald, and for over forty years they enjoyed a unique relationship as a husband and wife who successfully pursued separate writing careers.

She published her first novel, *The Invisible Worm*, in 1941. Now, over four decades later, she is busily polishing her twenty-fifth work of fiction. During that time she has established herself as one of the great practitioners in the field of mystery and psychological suspense. Her work has been translated into more than a dozen foreign languages, appeared in twenty-seven paperback editions and has been selected seventeen times by book clubs. She received an Edgar Award for the Best Mystery of the Year with her classic *Beast In View;* and two of her other novels, *The Fiend* and *How Like an Angel,* were runners-up for that award. She is a past President of the Mystery Writers of America, and in 1983 she received that organization's most prestigious honor, the Grand Master Award, for lifetime achievement.